A Christmas Kiss on the Twenty-Fifth

KATHRYN KALEIGH

THE DEVEREAUXS

(Reading Order)

Red Lipstick Kisses and Small Town Wishes

Stolen Dances and Big City Chances

Chance Connections and Upside Down Plans

A Christmas Kiss on the Twenty-Fifth

Believe in the Magic of Christmas

ALSO BY KATHRYN KALEIGH

Contemporary Romance

Belonging in Alpine Falls

Stranded in Alpine Falls

Believe in the Magic of Christmas

The Princess and the Playboy

A Christmas Kiss on the Twenty-Fifth

Red Lipstick Kisses and Small Town Wishes

Stolen Chances and Big City Chances

Chance Connections and Upside Down Plans

Accidentally Forever

Finding Forever

Forever Vows

Our Forever Love

My Forever Guy

Out of the Blue

Kissing for Keeps

All Our Tomorrows

Pretend Boyfriend

The Forever Equation

A Chance Encounter

Chasing Fireflies

When Cupid's Arrow Strikes

It was Always You

On the Way Home to Christmas

A Merry Little Christmas

On the Way to Forever

Perfectly Mismatched

The Moon and the Stars at Christmas

Still Mine

Borrowed Until Monday

The Lady in the Red Dress

On the Edge of Chance

Sealed with a Kiss

Kiss me at Midnight

The Heart Knows

Billionaire's Unexpected Landing

Billionaire's Accidental Girlfriend

Billionaire Fallen Angel

Billionaire's Secret Crush

Billionaire's Barefoot Bride

The Heart of Christmas

The Magic of Christmas

In a One Horse Open Sleigh

A Secret Royal Christmas

An Old-Fashioned Christmas

Second Chance Kisses

Second Chance Secrets

First Time Charm

Three Broken Rules

Second Chance Destiny

Unexpected Vows

Begin Again

Love Again

Falling Again

Just Stay

Just Chance

Just Believe

Just Us

Just Once

Just Happened

Just Maybe

Just Pretend

Just Because

A Christmas Kiss on the Twenty-Fifth

Chapter One

Genevieve Devereaux

Stepping out of the elevator, being pulled along behind two snow white Husky puppies, one leash in each hand, I wondered why I hadn't changed out of my high heels before picking up my neighbor's dogs.

The valet opened the door leading out to the dog walk as the puppies neared the door ahead of me.

"Thank you, Jose," I said as I followed the dogs through the door.

"It's chilly out there, Miss Genevieve," Jose said. "You forget your coat again, yes?"

"Yes. Hopefully they'll be fast."

"You have the optimism," Jose said. "But let me take them out for you."

"No. No. It's okay." But the cold air struck my skin, tempting me to let Jose take the dogs.

Instead, I released the tension on their leashes and let them run. Holly and Molly. That's what Mrs. Miller had named her dogs. She claimed her five-year-old twin granddaughters named them on a Zoom call. The way she doted on those grandkids, I had no doubt it was the truth.

White clouds hung low, making it look more like eight o'clock than just four o'clock.

I walked along the railing of the third-floor dog park of my condo building. From here I had a good view of Post Oak and 610.

Festive decorations lined Post Oak Boulevard. Hundreds of twenty-feet tall metal Christmas trees glowing with lights—green, then red, then silver and back around again, this time adding blue to the mix.

Bumper to bumper traffic right on schedule. Buses blocking traffic on the outside lane. Traffic backed up at the intersections. I worked from home three days a week, but on Mondays and Wednesdays I had to go in to the office. Fortunately, I usually made it home before the traffic locked up.

Mrs. Miller, my neighbor across the hall, had broken her ankle two weeks ago and I had taken up the job of taking care of her pets.

She had a daughter who lived in California—I'd met her a couple of times—who was travel restricted with expecting a new baby, not to mention her five-year-old twins, to come home to tend to her mother. Mrs. Miller also had a son who lived in Pittsburgh, but I'd never met him in the six months I'd known Mrs. Miller.

She talked constantly about both of them. Bragged about how her daughter was a good mother and an accountant. She talked about how her son was a pilot for Skye Travels.

I hadn't known that Skye Travels had a location in Pittsburgh.

They were a Houston company founded by the legendary Noah Worthington. I'd read that he had started Skye Travels with one little Cessna airplane and had grown it into the largest private airline company in the country.

I had three aviation students that I knew of who had gone through my classes who had applied to work for Skye Travels. Two of them had gotten interviews and one of them had gotten hired.

Apparently it was quite competitive and, according to my students, Noah Worthington personally interviewed anyone who got hired.

Holly, I knew it was Holly because she wore a green plaid collar with a bow nipped at Molly's heels. Molly, wearing a blue plaid collar, was more sedate. By herself, Molly would have been a quiet easy-going puppy, but together the twins were a handful.

I found it interesting that the puppies, like human twins, had personalities on opposite ends of the spectrum. I'd used the puppies as an example just this morning in my Developmental psychology class when I'd talked about twins.

I shivered as a gust of wind whipped around the side of the building and tossed my hair into my face. Jose had been right. It was too cold to be out here.

I tugged at their leashes, urging them to hurry up and do their business, but they didn't seem interested. Being Huskies, they thrived in the cold weather.

Maybe I would round them up and come back later after I put on my wool coat.

This was Houston. It wasn't supposed to be this cold.

Houston had two seasons. Hot and less hot.

Besides, it was only the middle of December. The cold weather didn't normally make any kind of appearance until January.

If it was going to be cold, though, I preferred it be cold around Christmas. It was rare for Houston to have cold weather at the holidays. I found that to be unfortunate. If I could move up north, I would, but my family was here. Well, not here as in Houston, but in a small town just north of Houston. Maple Creek.

"Two more minutes," I called out to the dogs. Not that they listened or cared.

In fact, they obviously had no interest in going back inside.

I walked back toward the door and found a spot that was, at least, somewhat out of the wind while I waited.

Jose opened the door and made a loud whistle.

The two dogs, obviously understanding a dog whistle when they heard it, raced toward the door.

I followed.

"Thank you, Jose," I said.

Jose handed them each a dog treat.

"Where did you get those?"

"I brought them from home," he said. "My dogs. They eat too much. So they share."

"I owe you one," I said.

"Just wear your coat next time. We call it even."

The dogs followed Jose—their new best friend—to the elevator and we rode back up to Mrs. Miller's condo.

I had left the door unlocked. The building's ironclad security made it impossible for anyone who didn't live on the twenty-fifth floor to get anywhere near it.

There were only four units on the floor and one was vacant. Besides me and Mrs. Miller, the other one belonged to a pro baseball player who was rarely home.

I thought of the twenty-fifth floor as our own little neighborhood. Each floor was a neighborhood and the condo building itself was a little town.

Having grown up in a small town, it was how I made sense of the building community.

I moved quietly even though Mrs. Miller was in the back of the condo in her bedroom and couldn't hear me.

I unhooked Molly. Then Holly. As they raced toward the back of the condo toward the bedroom, I hung up their leashes by the door. Mrs. Miller had crutches, but spent most of her time, when she wasn't in physical therapy, in her bedroom.

It was time to feed everyone. That meant the two dogs and Mrs. Miller's two cats. I was a little more friendlier with the two cats. For one, I'd been introduced to them when I first met Mrs. Miller, before she got the puppies. And second, my grandmother had a cat.

Our parents hadn't allowed us to have pets growing up, but I had bonded enough with Grandma's cat to tell me that I was a cat person.

Not that I disliked dogs. Everyone, it seemed, had an innate preference for one over the other. Cats versus dogs.

I walked toward the kitchen, my heels landing quietly on the carpet, wondering where the two cats were. They usually raced to meet me in the kitchen when it was time to eat.

I turned the corner and squealed, literally jumping backwards.

A man stood in Mrs. Miller's kitchen on the other side of the island.

I'd never seen this man before. The glimpse I had of him told me that he was dressed in black.

The bad guys always wore black.

Somehow from the time I had taken the dogs down to the park, frozen my tail off, then brought the dogs back upstairs, someone had slipped into Mrs. Miller's condo.

Instinctively reaching for the cell phone that hung on a strap around my neck, I took a step back.

"Wait," the man said. "I'm James."

My hands shook as I fumbled with my phone. No one could get here in time to help us. It was just me and Mrs. Miller.

Letting my phone fall to my side, I reached out blindly. Grasped the first thing my fingers touched.

An umbrella. I grabbed the long stadium umbrella and held it up in front of me like a weapon.

The man didn't move. He just looked at me with an amused expression.

"I'm James," he said again.

James.

I didn't know anyone named James.

I took another step back.

He didn't look dangerous.

At least not dangerous in a bad way. Maybe actually dangerous in a good sort of way.

He was tall and lean. Dark hair that just barely brushed the top of his collar. He had what looked like one of those expensive haircuts that guys got every week or so.

Other than wearing a black leather jacket, he didn't look like a dangerous criminal.

That could explain how he got past security. He looked clean-cut and successful.

And his smile was disarming.

"How did you get in here?" I asked.

"The door was unlocked," he said.

This was my fault. I had left the door unlocked.

"Come now," he said. "Are you going to hit me with that umbrella?"

"Maybe," I said, realizing how ridiculous I must look.

"You're Genevieve."

I looked at him sideways. Adrenalin rushed through my system.

"I'm James Miller."

"Miller. You're..."

"Peggy Miller is my mother."

I slowly lowered the umbrella.

"James Miller."

"Yes." A smiled played about his lips.

"Mrs. Miller didn't tell me you were coming." I tried to think. To put it all together, but he was throwing me off guard with his glacier blue eyes.

"I know," he said. "It was a surprise."

"Oh." I slowly set the umbrella back where I'd found it and straightened, attempting to look dignified although I felt anything but.

In fact, I felt quite foolish.

"Well. I'm certain your mother is very happy to see you."

"She is."

"I'll just go now."

"She said you would know where the cat food is."

Of course I knew where the cat food was.

He was standing on the other side of the island right in front of the cabinet where she kept the canisters.

"It's right there," I said.

He held up his hands, looking quite helpless and innocent.

"Okay. I'm here to feed them anyway."

He looked so relieved, it was almost comical.

This day most certainly wasn't going the way I had expected it to.

Chapter Two

James

Even though my mother's kitchen reminded me of the home I had grown up in, this condo on the twenty-fifth floor of a luxury high rise building was nothing like the house in the suburbs where I had grown up.

It had been me, my sister, and our parents.

Father had passed away two years ago after being sick for three years.

He'd actually helped her sell their house and move here before he passed away.

It had been quite disconcerting to be around them during that time.

So I had done what most adult children would do.

I had stayed away.

In fact, since my father got sick, I only visited for a few days at Christmas. We were coming up on year seven when I rarely came home.

But as soon as my sister had told me about my mother's broken ankle, I had gotten on a plane this way.

I figured I'd make sure she had appropriate caregivers, then head out.

My sister not only couldn't leave her children, but was restricted from flying due to pregnancy, and even though I worked all the time, I, at least, didn't have children to worry about.

My mother had tried to compress a five thousand square foot house down to a two thousand foot condo.

There was less furniture than we'd grown up with, but still, I had to navigate furniture to stand in front of one of the floor-to-ceiling windows to look outside.

Even though she had gotten rid of a lot of the furniture, most of her other belongings had made the cut.

I could tell by the closets bulging with clothes and other things.

The kitchen was no different.

The cabinets were strategically packed so that everything fit inside like pieces of a puzzle.

Personally, living like this would drive me insane. I needed blank walls where I could rest my eyes and I liked to be able to open up a cabinet and see everything inside at a glance.

It was baffling that I was so different from the rest of my family.

I did like her Christmas tree, all nine feet of it, tucked over in a corner by the television decorated with a lot of the old decorations we'd had as children. I was glad she had kept them. I had fond memories of our little family at Christmas time. Spending the day decorating the tree. Putting the angel on top.

When I'd gotten here, my mother had told me that the neighbor was out walking her dogs. Fortunately, my sister had warned me that Mother had adopted two puppies.

I had yet to understand what had possessed her to get more pets.

What I did know was that the puppies were the very reason she had a broken ankle.

She had gotten up in the middle of the night and tripped over one of the dogs. Or at least that was the version of the story I had gotten from my sister.

My mother had yet to admit to it. She could be quite evasive.

When Mother had told me that the neighbor was walking the dogs, she had neglected to tell me that the neighbor was a green-eyed goddess with flowing brunette hair who wielded an umbrella like a sword.

She, her name was Genevieve, walked right up to the island, opened one of the cabinets, and pulled out a canister of cat food.

Both of Mother's cats, appeared at her feet on cue.

Genevieve knelt down, filled the two cats bowls, and rubbed the cats' backs.

"Thank you," I said.

Closing the lid on the canister, she looked up at me with amusement.

She was adorable whether she was wielding an umbrella like a sword or kneeling next to the cats.

"Can I help you up?" I asked, holding out a hand.

She looked at me a moment, then put a hand in mine.

She didn't need my help to stand up. She was light as a feather and graceful as a ballerina, even on two inch heels.

But once she was on her feet, I didn't want to let her go.

I was a full head taller than she was, even with the heels. I didn't have to pull her close against me to know that she was the perfect height for me.

"Do you want to come back?" I asked. "Talk to Mother?"

"I know you two have a lot of catching up to do," she said. "I'll just let myself out."

She pulled her hand from mine and, after returning the canister to the cabinet, went around the island.

"It's nice to finally meet you," she said. "I've heard a lot about you."

"I wish I could say the same," I said. "Maybe I should talk to my mother more often."

"She would definitely love that. I'm sure I'll see you around," she said.

And then she was gone.

I stood frozen in place, the two cats eating noisily at my feet.

My mother had most definitely withheld important information from me.

Chapter Three

Genevieve

I walked across the hall, let myself into my own condo, and went straight to the kitchen.

Since I went home for Christmas, I didn't do a lot of decorating. I didn't even have a tree. This was my first Christmas living away from home and I didn't have all that quite figured out yet, but I was regretting not putting up a tree. Maybe next year. Definitely next year.

While I waited for the water in the electric tea kettle to heat, I stepped out of my heels, and removed my phone from its strap around my neck.

It was a great way to carry my phone when I was at the university, but not so much when I was at home.

Now that James was here, he could take the dogs out for their walks. He could feed the cats, too, now that I had showed him where his mother kept the cat food.

In a way, it was nice to be off the hook for however long he was here.

In another way, I was tempted to find an excuse to go back over there to see if Mrs. Miller needed anything else. Going back over there meant I would get to see James again.

I don't know what I was expecting, but somehow I hadn't expected James to be a handsome pilot who came across as the hapless son who didn't know how to feed his mother's cats.

Surely he could figure out how to feed his mother's pets.

Then again... he was related to the woman who had broken her ankle when she'd fallen over a puppy. Or two.

Mrs. Miller had never really told me just why she had gotten two dogs when she already had two cats. I just sort of figured she was lonely. Dogs most definitely required a lot more moving about including several trips a day downstairs.

To make sure I didn't go back across the hall, I changed into sweatpants, a t-shirt, and a hoody. It was how I signaled my brain that it was time to sit at my computer and get to work.

Comfortable now, I filled a mug with hot water, added a tea bag, and a spoonful of honey.

I had lectures to prepare. I didn't have time to waste hanging out with the neighbor's son, especially not when the neighbor's son lived in Pittsburgh.

I did know that she would be happy to see him. She talked about him all the time.

My parents were fortunate that their adult children all lived close. My oldest brother lived in Maple Creek with his wife while my next oldest brother and sister lived in the house with our parents.

It wasn't actually what most called a house. It was more like a manor. A manor with plenty of room for everyone to have their own suite.

My younger brother still lived at home and was still in college.

I was the only one who lived away from Maple Creek at the moment and I visited two or three times a month, depending on my schedule.

Sometimes, like this week, I had lots of lectures to prepare for and I had two final exams to make. The odds of me getting up to Maple Creek this weekend were looking quite slim.

I took my hot tea to my little office and sat down at my desk looking out toward downtown Houston. The floor to ceiling windows gave me a clear view of downtown. The skyscrapers, though, were so far away they looked like a little stack of brightly lit children's blocks from here.

With the mug warming my hands, I watched a jet circle around and start its descent into the airport north of town.

Sometimes my view was right in the flight path. Sometimes not.

I didn't see very many smaller jets from here, though. They must use a different route.

That was something I could ask James if I saw him again.

The odds of seeing him again, though, were next to nothing.

I'd be in my condo tomorrow working, then I'd be at the university on Wednesday teaching my face-to-face classes.

By then James would probably be gone.

According to Mrs. Miller, her son, and her daughter, for that matter, rarely stayed more than a few days. In fact, she had told me that James only came home for Christmas. That explained why I didn't catch on to who he was. I had accepted that since I spent Christmas week every year in Maple Creek and James only came home at Christmas, we would never cross paths.

She claimed she didn't mind that her children rarely visited. Understood that they were busy with their lives. But I could tell that she did mind. That she missed them terribly and wished they came to visit more often.

I think she'd been planning a trip to California to visit her daughter and family when she'd broken her ankle. That was before I'd started walking her dogs and I hadn't known her as well then. She'd mentioned something about planning to board her pets.

I understood the sentiment. My parents used to complain about our brother Jonathan. Jonathan had rarely come home.

Then, just like that, he'd met Sophia and moved back to Maple Creek.

Now that they could see him all the time, our parents no longer acted like he was their favorite. With five children they naturally favored the one who never came home.

As I turned on my computer and opened up the textbook chapter I needed to review and summarize, I thought about James.

I felt guilty when I only visited my family once a month. How could James go a whole year without visiting his mother? And to make matters worse, he was a pilot. There were three pilots in my family so I was pretty sure it wasn't possible to be a pilot and not see the world as a much smaller place than the rest of us.

Pilots hopped on airplanes and flew across the country at the drop of a hat. Taking a flight was for them like driving across town for the rest of us.

I tried to give him a break, giving him excuses like his mother did, but I couldn't do it. I couldn't help feeling bad for Mrs. Miller that her pilot son only came to visit her once a year.

He was here now.

And it wasn't my business.

What James Miller did or didn't do wasn't my concern or my business.

I'd been working for a good hour when my attention was drawn to hallway toward the sound of barking dogs.

Chapter Four

James

I stood outside my mother's condo door.

The wide hallway and plush carpet muffled most of the sounds, but it couldn't muffle the sounds of the two Husky puppies barking. Holly and Molly. Only a five-year-old would name two dogs who looked exactly alike Holly and Molly.

I had the right condo. I was certain of it. 2501. I reached into my pocket to check my mother's address in my phone.

And discovered that I had left my phone inside the condo.

I tried the door again.

Even turned the knob and pushed against it with my shoulder.

It was most definitely locked. Mother had told me to leave it unlocked when I took the dogs downstairs. Apparently living on the twenty-fifth floor was supposed to be like living in a small town in the 1950s. Nobody locked their doors.

As far as I was concerned, there would never be enough security for me to feel safe leaving my door unlocked, no matter where I was.

Had I accidentally locked it out of habit when I had taken the dogs out?

It was quite possible, I mused.

The problem was that I didn't have a key.

And not only did I not have a key, but my mother was on the other side of the condo. If I knocked, she wouldn't hear me.

I didn't see a doorbell.

If I had my phone, I could call her to come open the door.

She had crutches. I hadn't seen her use them yet, but she'd told me that she could. She could use the crutches, but she couldn't use them to take the dogs outside. That's what she told me. The crutches, still new with tags, had rested against her dresser across the room from her bed. I hadn't asked.

And now I was in a mess.

The dogs stood at the closed door, barking.

Apparently, they knew they were in the right place and when they weren't barking their heads off, they were looking at me like something was wrong with me.

"I don't have a key," I told them out loud.

One of them, I don't know which, turned her head and looked at me, then went back to barking. Obviously not having a key was not a sufficient answer.

The door across the hall opened and Genevieve stood there looking at me questioningly. I'd never been so glad to see someone.

Her dark hair swirled around her shoulders and she looked comfortable in sweatpants, a hoody, and a pair of Uggs boots for slippers.

"Hi," I said.

"Hi."

"I don't have a key."

"Is the door locked?" she asked.

I made a face that said why else would I be standing out here in the hallway with two barking puppies.

As she stepped across the hall and tried the door herself, I noticed that she smelled like lavender.

"It's locked," she said.

"I know." The dogs were sitting quietly now, watching her. "Do you have a key?"

"No," she said, looking thoughtfully at the doorknob. "I should though, shouldn't I?"

"It seems like someone should." I didn't mean for it to sound accusatory. It wasn't her fault she didn't have a key to my mother's condo. If anyone should have a key, it should be me.

"You're right," she said, looking at me now. "Someone should."

She had green eyes that reminded me of a sparkling verdant forest after a rain.

Without her high heels, she looked smaller, more delicate. Like a fairy princess.

"Why are you smiling?" she asked, crossly.

"I'm not smiling," I said, placing a hand over my face as I realized that I was, indeed, smiling.

She nodded slowly, then looked back at the door. She turned

away from me, but not before I saw the play of a grin at the corner of her lips.

We were grinning like a couple of loons for no reason whatsoever.

In fact, we should be quite upset. I was locked out of my mother's condo. No key. With her two puppies.

"You can't stand out here all night," she said, turning. The dogs followed her.

Reaching her door, she stopped and looked over her shoulder. The dogs stopped and turned, too.

"Are you coming?"

"I guess I am."

I stepped through the door into Genevieve's condo and I knew I was in love.

Her condo was about the same size as my mother's, but it looked so much bigger.

She had a sofa and an oversized chair with an ottoman.

No television on the wall.

No pictures on the walls.

A bookcase with a few books.

But mostly, it was a minimalist's dream home.

"Nice," I said.

"It's a wonderful view of downtown," she said, thinking I was referring to the view.

I walked to the window and looked out. Floor to ceiling windows. Just like my mother had. But I could walk right up to the windows and look out without having to navigate furniture.

"I'll be right back," she said.

The dogs followed her.

I understood. I'd follow her, too, if I could.

Chapter Five

GENEVIEVE

I double-checked to make sure I had saved my work on the computer, then powered it down.

Molly and Holly had followed and sat at my feet, looking up at me.

"What are you guys doing in here?" I asked.

They just looked at me with their big puppy dog eyes.

"Come on," I said. "Let's go figure out how to get you home."

Taking my empty tea mug with me, I left my office, the two dogs following along at my heels.

I dropped off the mug in the kitchen, then went back into the living room where James waited. He sat on the chair in front of the window. The one where I liked to sit in the evenings when I had time to read for fun. Lately, though, it seemed like all I'd been reading was textbooks.

I went to the couch and sat down. The two dogs jumped up to sit one on either side of me.

"Come on, Dogs," James said. "Off the furniture."

"They're okay," I said. "You don't know their names, do you?"

"I do know their names. One is Molly and one is Holly."

"This one is Molly," I said, putting a hand on Molly's head. "She's a sweetie. And this one." I put a hand on Holly's head. "This is Holly. She wears green like Christmas holly and she's festive. She's energetic and festive."

"Huh. I don't think I'll ever have trouble forgetting which is which again. As long as they're wearing their collars at least."

"Then I did a good job."

"How do you do it?"

"It's my super power."

"Mother told me you're a professor. So it's a good super power for you to have."

"It comes in handy."

"Beautiful, smart, and modest."

"And you're bold." And charming and handsome. But I wasn't ready to tell him that.

I was familiar enough with pilots to figure he didn't need any help swelling up his head with compliments.

He grinned as though he knew what I didn't say as well as what I did say.

"What are we going to do about your predicament?" I asked.

"You have my mother's phone number?"

"I don't have a key, but I do have her phone number." I pulled my phone out of my pocket. "Good place to start."

I dialed Mrs. Miller's number.

"What is it?" he asked when I frowned.

"Straight to voicemail."

"This keeps getting better by the minute."

"Does she usually turn her phone off?"

"I don't think so," he said, having the decency to look guilty.

"We'll try her again in a few minutes."

"Not to be negative," he said. "But if she doesn't answer…"

"If she doesn't answer," I said. "You're going to have a long night."

"Not funny."

"She has crutches, right?"

"Yes. But I haven't seen her use them."

"Neither have I."

Molly crawled over my lap and curled up next to Holly. Mrs. Miller had been smart to get both puppies. They were adorable together.

"I don't even know if she can use them," he said. "to be quite honest with you."

"Let's stay positive and assume she can use her crutches."

He nodded slowly, obviously not convinced that this was helpful.

"They would have taught her in the hospital."

He nodded again. "They still have their tags on them and they were across the room from her bed."

"Right," I said. "Probably not so good."

We sat in silence for a couple of minutes. The train rumbled past outside, far, far below.

"How long have you lived here?" he asked.

"Six months."

"It's nice. Spacious."

"Thanks.

"My mom thinks I need to decorate."

"Yeah. I get that response sometimes, too."

"Do you? You're a minimalist?"

"Pretty much. I got tired of moving stuff."

"You moved around a lot?"

"A couple of places here in Houston after I left home. Then I've moved twice since I moved to Pittsburgh."

"That's a lot of moving. You moved from The Woodlands, right?"

"Yeah. The move to Pittsburgh taught me that I didn't need a lot to be happy. Have you moved a lot?"

"Just once. I moved here from my parents' house. I didn't have a lot to bring."

"You're lucky."

"I am. Can I get you something to drink? I have hot tea and water. I can make some coffee."

"Just some water," he said.

The puppies had fallen asleep, curled up together.

"I'll get it."

I needed to think of how to resolve this problem, but it was hard to think sitting here with James.

He distracted me.

Chapter Six

James

The dogs, Holly and Molly, slept peacefully on Genevieve's sofa. They looked right at home here and, I had to admit, I felt at home, too.

Genevieve's condo smelled clean like vanilla and maybe a hint of cinnamon.

It was spacious, but oddly enough, it wasn't stark. She had a couple of accent pillows and a clock on the mantle. A succulent. Little things that weren't noticeable at first, but provided just enough décor to make it homey.

I sat in the chair across from the sofa where the dogs slept.

Genevieve handed me a glass of ice water and went back to the sit on the sofa.

"So," she said. "I have an idea."

"What's that?"

"We call the concierge. See if they can unlock the door."

"Ah. They should have keys, shouldn't they?"

I had always lived in a house, so my knowledge of the workings of a high rise were a bit lacking.

"They might. If she leased it, they definitely would, but she owns it, right?"

"Yes," I said. That much I knew for certain. I remembered my parents talking about the advantages and disadvantages of owning a condo. My father had insisted that they purchase it outright so that Mother never had to worry about paying rent.

"I'll give them a call," she said.

I listened as she spoke to the concierge.

Our gazes met and held as she talked. Her eyes were so expressive I could almost follow the conversation just by watching her.

After a few minutes, she disconnected the line.

"What did he say?"

"He has to check on it."

"Wait," I said. "Do they have a key or not?"

"They do have a key. If they could talk to her, it wouldn't be a problem, but since she doesn't answer the phone, the only way they can justify it is to make it an emergency."

"It might be an emergency."

"Well," she said. "It's a judgment call. He has to check with someone else."

"What a mess. I'll definitely be getting a key made."

"It didn't occur to me that no one had a key."

"Me either." And why would it? I wasn't here. As far as I was concerned, my mother was here, living safely in her condo.

And then when I learned otherwise—about her ankle—that's when I got here as soon as I could. Unfortunately, my mother didn't tell me and my sister waited two weeks.

I would be having words with my sister, for sure.

"So we just wait?"

"He's going to call me back," she said, idly running a hand over the Molly's fur. "Do you have pets?"

"Me? No. I don't have anything tying me down."

"Oh. I'm sorry."

"You don't have pets," I said, in my own defense.

"No. But I have family."

"You have children?" I sounded a whole lot calmer asking that question than I felt.

"No. Not that kind of family. Parents. Brothers. Sisters. I'm going to be an aunt soon."

"I'm an uncle."

"Right. And you're about to be an uncle again."

"They live so far away," I said. "Sometimes I don't think it counts."

I hadn't even realized that until right now, having said it out loud.

"It counts," Genevieve said. "It's one of those things that will always count."

"Good point."

"Are you more of a dog person or a cat person?" she asked, scratching Molly's ears.

"I don't know."

"You have to know. If you don't know, you'd be the first person who didn't."

"Maybe I like both."

"You can like both," she said. "But most people have some kind of preference."

"Dogs," I said. Guys preferred dogs. Girls liked cats. "What about you?"

"Cats," she said. Then smiled. "But I like both."

"The dogs like you."

"They like everybody," she said.

I didn't bother to point out that she was the one they were sitting with. She was the one they followed around.

Again, though, I noted her modesty.

It was one of those traits that was sorely lacking in the women I met these days.

Maybe I'd been looking in the wrong place.

Chapter Seven

GENEVIEVE

Living on the twenty-fifth floor took some getting used to.

It was quiet, especially so for a small-town girl like me. A lot of nights back home I'd crack my window to not only let in a little fresh air, but also to let in the night sounds. Crickets chirping. Owls hooting. Dogs barking.

Up here on the twenty-fifth floor I could hear the train when it rumbled past a few times a day. I could hear sirens when they passed by. Ambulances. Fire trucks. Police cars.

Sometimes I'd hear the gentle music of the pianist from one of the floors above me. I felt fortunate to have a concert pianist for a neighbor and not someone who played loud rock music. I'd heard stories.

I didn't have a television hanging on the wall of my living

room. The only time I watched movies or anything else on television for fun was when I visited my family in Maple Creek. Anything else I watched was for work and that's what my iPad was for.

Sitting here in my living room, the glow from a full moon hanging low coming through my window, two dogs curled up on my sofa, would have been relaxing.

But it was impossible to be relaxed with James Miller sitting in my favorite chair. He looked relaxed on the surface, but just beneath that surface, he seemed tense and on alert.

It was possible, however, that I was projecting.

I felt my own coil of tension just below the surface.

Other than my family, I didn't have a lot of visitors, and truth be told, even my family rarely visited me here. Mostly when I saw my family, I saw them in Maple Creek.

We were all in that phase of life when we were busy with our careers. My three older siblings were also busy making families of their own.

I hadn't gotten to that particular phase. My high school boyfriend and I had broken up during the summer after graduation. We'd gone our separate ways with no hard feelings.

Other than that, I had dated a fellow graduate student my first year of my doctoral program. We had been what my mother called attached at the hip.

But then when our second year started and the new first-year students came in, he moved into the role of mentor with one of those students.

Long story short, they were married now.

Making the decision not to date anyone else in psychology had been a good decision, but since psychology was all I did, I didn't meet anyone else.

Putting my head down and focusing had been good for my career.

But I couldn't remember the last time I had sat alone in a room with a guy I wasn't related to or who wasn't a client or student.

I made friends easily, my neighbors and the staff at the building included.

That's how I ended up here. Being friends with my neighbor across the hall.

So much for not seeing James again. He'd left his phone in her condo when he'd taken the dogs out for their walk and now he was locked out.

As we waited for the concierge to call back, I wondered what we were going to do if they refused to open Mrs. Miller's door.

Since her phone was off, it was impossible to say for sure whether or not she was in an emergency situation. They had to ere on the side of caution and let James inside the condo.

In the unlikely event that they did not, he could stay in my guest room.

"Penny for your thoughts," he said.

"Excuse me?"

"It's an old saying. You look deep in thought."

I straightened in my seat.

"I was just thinking that you can stay in my guest room."

"That's kind of you. But let's hope it doesn't come to that."

"Right. I was just thinking through all the possibilities."

"They have to consider that she could have fallen and can't get to her phone or to the door."

"That's what I was just thinking."

"We could call a locksmith."

"I thought of that," I said, shaking my head. "I think you have to show some kind of proof to get in, don't you?"

"I don't know. This is a first for me."

"Hmm. Me too."

"How long do you think it'll be before they call?"

"I don't know."

I tried calling Mrs. Miller again.

Still straight to voicemail.

I looked over at James and shrugged.

"We could call your sister."

"We could. But I don't have her number either."

It looked like James and I were on our own.

His blue eyes locked onto mine and I couldn't read his expression. I considered myself fairly good at reading other people, but I couldn't read his expression.

"I'll go make sure the guest room is ready," I said.

Chapter Eight

Jᴀᴍᴇꜱ

Moonlight streamed in through the window along with lights from the city.

It was cold tonight. Unseasonably cold for Houston. Pittsburgh, on the other hand, had already had its first snowfall of the season.

It wasn't in the official forecast, but I was predicting snow for Houston. Maybe tomorrow or tomorrow night. It was that cold and the clouds looked prime for snow.

I'd left my heavy coat in the Lear jet I had flown in on.

Genevieve seemed fidgety.

She couldn't sit more than a few minutes before she'd think of an excuse to get up again.

Molly lifted her head when Genevieve got up, but didn't move to get up.

As long as the dogs were quiet, we were okay. If they got hungry, we were going to be in trouble.

Maybe I should drive somewhere and get some dog food. It didn't, however, seem necessary because they had just eaten before I took them out for their walk.

I'd spent the hour after Genevieve left sitting on a chair in my mother's bedroom while she talked to her granddaughters on a Zoom call.

They tried to include me, but I mostly just sat in the background and watched.

Mother had been talking to them on her computer. I hadn't noticed where her phone was, much less if it was on or off.

She'd been sitting in her bed at the time and was probably there now. Probably asleep even.

She would have no way of knowing what she was putting me through.

Other than worrying about what I was going to do about the predicament, it wasn't a hardship. Not when I was here getting to know Genevieve.

I was intrigued by her.

She really was beautiful and smart. And she didn't seem to even know it.

That was one of the things that added to her charm.

I watched traffic flowing up and down the streets outside, the steady flicker of headlights.

A helicopter flew past and I watched as it landed on one of the nearby high rises.

Since I had never lived in this area of Houston, I couldn't say what kind of building it was. A hotel maybe?

Genevieve came back from the bedrooms, her phone in her hand.

"The concierge called," she said. "They're going to open your mom's door for you."

"Oh. That's great news," I said, standing up. And if it was such great news, why did I feel so disappointed?

"They're on their way up now."

"I should go, then," I said. "Meet them over there."

"Right," she said, glancing down at the dogs. "Just go check on her. Leave the dogs here. You can come back and get them."

"Okay," I said. It was silly that the prospect of coming back over here, even if it was just to pick up the puppies had me feeling so happy.

"I'll be back in a few minutes," I said.

She followed me to the door and waited with me.

"It's Jose," she said when a young man stepped off the elevator. "Thanks so much, Jose, for coming up and doing this."

"You know I don't mind," Jose said. "How are you, Mr. James? We will get you right in."

He put the key in the lock and opened it right up.

"It works a lot better with a key," James said.

"Good night," Jose said with a little wave as he headed back to the elevator. "I will see you both tomorrow."

"I'll be back for the dogs," James told me.

"Take your time," Genevieve said. "I'll leave my door unlocked for you."

"Ha. Ha. Good one."

I could add funny to her list of attributes.

Chapter Nine

GENEVIEVE

I paced my condo while I waited for James to come back.

The puppies slept through the whole thing. It was amazing to me how they had so much energy one minute, then slept so soundly the next.

I stopped at the door to my guest room. I kept it ready for unexpected guests. Anytime my brothers or sisters came into town, they were welcome to stay here. My grandmother had spent the night here once even though she had a place of her own in the city.

My family was nothing if not supportive and with me being the youngest girl in the family, I had plenty of people watching after me.

I liked my little guest room. It had a full sized bed with white bedding, a plush comforter. There was a dresser with nothing on it but a vase that I used for fresh flowers when I knew someone would be staying over and a chair with an ottoman in front of the window. The chair was a smaller version of the one in my living room.

I enjoyed the view from my windows and I liked it when others were able to enjoy it, too.

Walking back into my living room, I sat down on the chair James had been sitting in.

It was unusual for someone to appreciate what a lot of people called my stark decorating tendencies.

I don't know where I learned it, but I liked things clean and spacious. No one else in my family seemed to have the same tendencies.

James, however, seemed to like it.

He was certainly different from his mother in that respect.

Mrs. Miller had explained how she had downsized from a big house in the Woodlands when she had moved here.

It seemed to me that she had brought everything with her and maybe even added a few things, but of course, I hadn't seen her house before she moved.

She had a nice view of the west side of Houston, but it was hard to get near a window to really appreciate it. One had to appreciate her view for the most part from the middle of the room.

It didn't bother me. I just didn't want to live like that.

I checked my phone. I had a message from my older sister reminding me that our mother's birthday was in two weeks and since it just happened to fall on a Saturday, the Saturday before Christmas, we were throwing a little party at her house that day.

First of all, I wouldn't forget it. And second of all, I had it set on my phone's calendar. I couldn't remember ever forgetting a family member's birthday.

I jumped when James knocked at the door.

"Come in," I said. It had to be him.

"Hey," he said, opening the door.

"Hey. How's your mother?"

"Would you believe that she was asleep?"

I laughed. "Yes. Yes, I would."

"She had no idea what was going on."

"Aw. It's okay."

"She's lucky to have you as a neighbor," he said. "I'll just take these puppies off your hands."

"You know what," I said. "They look so peaceful. I can bring them over when they wake up."

He gave me a quizzical look.

"Unless, of course, you have other plans," I added quickly.

"I don't have any other plans," he said. "It's just you've already gone above and beyond."

"I don't mind. I was just going to sit and read for a bit. I usually go over and take them out for a walk before I go to bed anyway."

"Now you're just making me look bad." He gave me a sheepish grin.

"I don't really think that's possible."

After he left, leaving the dogs behind, I sat down on my

reading chair and picked up the book I'd been reading, but I didn't open it.

Instead, I ran a hand over the foiled cover and looked over at the puppies sleeping soundly.

My evening had most definitely been unexpected.

And now I couldn't stop thinking about James Miller.

Chapter Ten

I spent the hour waiting for Genevieve to bring the puppies home flipping through channels on the television. Somehow every commercial had to do with Christmas. I finally settled on a romantic Christmas movie.

I thought about calling Angela, but it was too late.

It was an hour later in Pittsburgh and for all I knew she had an early flight tomorrow.

We weren't dating. Not exactly.

I guess technically we were dating, but not exclusively. And not to the point that we knew each other's schedules.

The truth was, I didn't want to talk to Angela right now.

I flipped channels again and glanced toward the door.

What I really wanted to do was to go back over and see Genevieve.

I did not, however, have a good excuse to do so.

Ten minutes later, she knocked on my mother's door.

Grabbing my jacket, I hurried to the door.

"Hi," I said, throwing it open.

"Hi."

Genevieve stood there, holding the two leashes, one in each hand. The puppies sat at her heels. Holly yawned.

"You're wearing your coat," I said. She had on a heavy black wool coat with black leather gloves.

"You're not."

"I left my coat on the plane."

"That's why I wore my coat," she said. "I can run them down."

"Why don't we both go?"

"Okay," she said with a little shrug.

I stepped out, but she held up a hand before I closed the door.

"Did you bring a key?"

I held up the key.

"Good thinking."

"Let me at least take one of them," I said as we waited for the elevator "So it looks like I'm doing something."

She laughed and handed me Holly's leash.

"And you gave me the difficult one."

"She's not really bad," Genevieve said, but when the elevator door opened, Holly raced ahead and got her leash tangled up with Molly's.

"Not bad, huh?" I got the puppies untangled and stood next to Genevieve as the elevator dropped to the third floor.

"Why is everything on the third floor?" I asked.

"I don't know. Security."

"Right. Security."

I wondered, but didn't ask, why they left their door unlocked when security was so important. She seemed to read my mind.

"It's how we don't have to worry once we reach our floor."

"Has anyone every told you that you're a little scary?"

"I'm not scary," she said, holding up a hand to wave at the concierge.

"Right."

With no valet there to open the door, I pushed it open myself and cringed at the cold air that slapped me in the face.

"Who would have thought it would be colder down here in Houston than it is in Pittsburgh?"

"You never know what you're going to find in Houston."

"No," I said, looking at her. "A truer statement was never spoken."

She smiled and released the tension on Molly's leash, letting the puppy run.

Genevieve Devereaux was like no one I had ever met.

Chapter Eleven

We'd only been outside for about five minutes when my teeth started chattering.

"It's seriously weirdly cold, even wearing my coat."

"You go inside," James said, holding out a hand for Molly's leash.

"No," I said. "I'm okay."

"You don't look okay. Can't have you getting hypothermia."

"I'm fine." But my teeth were chattering.

"Go," he said, taking the dog's leash.

I made a sound, but I wasn't going to keep arguing.

I went inside and watched him through the glass wall as I slowly began to warm.

It wasn't supposed to be this cold in November, was it? I couldn't remember it ever being this cold in November.

It wasn't long before James came inside, ushering the dogs along with him.

"Let's go up," he said. "I'll make you something hot to drink."

"I have hot tea."

"Since I have no idea what my mother has, we'll go with that."

"I'm going to drop these dogs off first," James said, as we got off the elevator on the twenty-fifth floor.

Back in my condo, I turned on the electric tea kettle and got down a couple of mugs while I waited for James.

I didn't know what to think about him.

Maybe, I decided, he was just being neighborly. Trying to make it up to me for taking care of his mother's pets.

It just didn't help that he was dangerously handsome. It was his eyes. His glacieral blue eyes had a way of grabbing hold of mine and not letting go.

Maybe it had something to do with him being a pilot. Two of my brothers and my brother-in-law were all pilots.

I considered myself immune to their uniform, which James wasn't even wearing, and I'd never been particularly partial to pilots. There was just something about James that had my heart racing whenever I looked at him.

"Come in," I said when he knocked at the door.

I busied myself with making our tea as he joined me.

I handed him a mug and wrapped my hands around mine.

Going back in my living room, I sat on the sofa and he sat down next to me.

"I think it's going to snow," he said.

"Not in Houston in November," I said. "I don't think it's possible."

"You want to make a wager?"

"What kind of wager?" I asked.

"If it snows, you have to take me to dinner."

"And if it doesn't?"

"Then I take you to dinner."

I laughed. "That sounds a bit fishy."

"Sounds like a win-win for me."

"Okay," I said. "It's a bet."

He held out a hand.

"Shake on it?"

Holding my mug in my left hand, I put my right hand in his.

It wasn't a handshake. It was more like a hand hold.

He held my hand in his and his eyes smiled into mine.

I didn't know whether to wish for snow of not.

It seemed like no matter which way it went I couldn't lose.

Chapter Twelve

I was having some pleasant dreams about a green-eyed girl named Genevieve when my phone started chiming with one text message after another.

I ignored it as long as I could, but the chiming finally penetrated my consciousness to the point where I could no longer ignore it.

Rolling over, I grabbed my phone and unlocked it.

NOAH WORTHINGTON

Do you have time to come up to the office sometime today?

NOAH WORTHINGTON

I know you're in Houston taking care of
your mother.

JOHN

Noah is trying to get in touch with you.
Not sure why.

Noah was what we called "the big boss." Noah was not only the owner of the company I worked for, Skye Travels, but he was also the founder. He had founded Skye Travels with just one little Cessna airplane. Skye Travels was now the largest private airline in the country.

John was my boss in Pittsburgh. The boss at the satellite location. He was responsible for making sure we all did our jobs, including making sure the scheduling got done and we followed through.

I wrote John back first.

He just texted me.

JOHN

I gave him your number.

What does he want?

JOHN

He didn't say.

Am I in trouble?

JOHN
For what?

Exactly.

Never know.

JOHN
Just go meet with him.

Meet with him? I scrolled back. That's what he'd said.

Why does he want to meet with me?

JOHN
Seriously James. He didn't tell me.

I obviously wasn't awake yet.

I decided to take a shower before writing "the big boss."

Ten minutes later, freshly showered, I felt a little more clear headed.

I can be there in an hour.

NOAH
No rush. Anytime today.

.   .   .

Might be no rush, but meeting with Noah Worthington was one of those things would worry me until I got it done.

Thirty minutes later, I was in an Uber heading toward the airport.

The Skye Travels offices were in a building right on the tarmac.

After the driver let me out in front of the building, I went up the elevator to the second floor.

The receptionist somehow knew who I was and ushered me right back to Noah's office.

He had one of those offices that would be the envy of not only any pilot, but the envy of anyone who liked to watch airplanes land and take off.

His view was like none I had ever seen.

"James," he said. "Thanks for taking the time to come up and meet with me."

"I'm glad I could," I said.

Noah was the one who had hired me to work for Skye Travels. He personally interviewed everyone who went to work for him.

I hadn't seen him since, but he wasn't the kind of man a person would forget. He was an impressive man at six feet tall. Steel gray hair. And an air of confidence and success that reflected the man he was.

"Come in," he said. "Have a seat."

I sat in one of three chairs in a little sitting area on side of his office, away from his big wooden desk.

"How's your mother?"

"She's good. Thank you for asking."

"Family always comes first," Noah said. "I'm glad to see you realize how important it is."

"Yes sir."

Noah handed me a bottle of water with the Skye Travels logo printed on the label.

"I asked you to come up here because I have a proposition for you."

Chapter Thirteen

Genevieve

The next day I holed up in my office and put together a test for my class.

The day was one of those cloudy days that just looked cold. According to my weather app, the temperature hovered around freezing, even dipping below now and again.

I should be happy about not having to go outside.

I had sent Mrs. Miller a text asking her to let me know if she needed anything.

She had sent back a quick agreement.

Since James was there with her, I worked under the assumption that he was taking care of her pets and anything else she might need.

I didn't want to intrude on their time together. I knew just how rare it was for James to get here for a visit.

In the last couple of weeks, it had become something of a routine for me to take her puppies out several times a day, so I rather missed doing it.

Just before noon, I received a message that face to face classes were cancelled tomorrow in anticipation of cold temperatures.

Not snow. Just cold temperatures.

I wanted it to snow.

It didn't make a lot of sense, though. My bet with James had me going to dinner with him either way.

I think I wanted it to snow because it was his prediction. I wanted him to be right.

As the day progressed, I admitted to myself that I liked James.

By mid-afternoon, I stared at my phone, wondering what kind of excuse I might have to contact Mrs. Miller.

No. I wasn't going to bother her. If she needed me, she would text.

I put my head down and got back to work.

When I looked up again, it was seven o'clock.

I didn't have any messages or calls, so I went to the kitchen and made myself a cheese sandwich.

I hadn't seen or heard from James all day.

He had forgotten.

That was the only explanation I could come up with.

Or maybe he had changed his mind.

Maybe he had come to his senses. Remembered that he lived in Pittsburgh and I lived here.

He only saw his own mother once a year. There was no reason

to think that he would make time to see a girl who lived in Houston, even if she did live across the hall from his mother.

Getting up, I turned on the tea kettle to make some tea.

A message from Mrs. Miller came in.

MRS. MILLER

Can you walk the puppies?

Of course. Now?

MRS. MILLER

Yes. James had to take a flight. I meant to ask you earlier, but I fell asleep.

I'll be right over.

I turned off the tea kettle.

So James had been called out to take a flight.

I hadn't even considered that explanation.

Somehow it made me feel about a hundred percent better.

He didn't have any way of contacting me so he couldn't have told me he was tied up with a flight even if he wanted to.

Not that he would have.

But a girl could dream.

Chapter Fourteen

Sometimes, like tonight, a man was reminded of best laid plans and all that.

Noah hadn't asked me to take what was supposed to be a quick flight up to Dallas. I had volunteered.

Part of what had tempted me was the chance to fly his brand new Phenom. What could I say? I was a pilot through and through.

Mother was fine. It was Tuesday and Tuesday was the day her caregiver came in to help her with her shower. I didn't need to be around for that anyway. Taking a flight was a good excuse to keep me away.

I'd made some calls and I was setting up some full time caregivers so she would have someone there all the time. If I'd known she needed them, I would have already done it. But, of course, I hadn't even known she had broken her ankle.

Another thing was she couldn't continue to impose on Genevieve for walking the puppies. It wasn't that Genevieve wasn't good with them. She obviously took good care of them, but it wasn't right to impose on her.

Mother had offered to pay Genevieve, but, of course, Genevieve wouldn't take any money.

I'd figure something out with that.

It was a fine line. She might be insulted if I hired a dog walker.

I stepped outside the hotel. Into the light falling snow.

Snow.

I'd flown right up into it and gotten stranded.

In a snowstorm.

It was almost a little bit funny.

This little bit of snow was just a normal every winter day in Pittsburgh. But here in Dallas, it shut the whole town down.

When I'd predicted snow, I'd predicted it for Houston and I still maintained that it was going to snow in Houston.

And finally, the forecasters had caught up and added a low possibility of snow to the Houston forecast.

Looked like Houston was shutting down, too. Just in case.

I walked along the sidewalk leading around the hotel. I was a little bit aggravated with myself for getting stranded here.

If I was going to get stranded somewhere, it would have been nice to have been stranded with Genevieve.

Wasn't that how it was supposed to go? That's how it happened in all the movies and romance books.

The hero and heroine would get stranded together and fall in love.

Not in real life, though, apparently.

In real life, the hero goes on a flight and gets stranded by himself while the heroine is left behind to walk his mother's dogs.

I stopped and looked up at the skies. Watched the thick snowflakes softly fluttering down.

It was no less than I deserved, was it?

I had been in a perfectly good position, spending time with my mother. Only to be lured away by the siren song of a phenom.

I would find a way to get out of here tomorrow.

To get back to Houston.

I wanted to spend time with Genevieve.

Chapter Fifteen

GENEVIEVE

I took utmost advantage of the extra day off to get some work done.

Right after I indulged in sleeping in.

I rarely slept in, even when I didn't have to drive to work, I still went to work. Teaching was one of those jobs that it was almost impossible to get ahead on. Not so different from most jobs, I mused.

Since it was Wednesday and I was supposed to be in class, I didn't have any clients all day.

After a hot shower, I went across the hall to take the dogs for their morning walk.

According to Mrs. Miller, James was stranded in Dallas where it was actually snowing.

I was pretty sure that even though it was snowing in Dallas where he was, that didn't count as a win for him.

Not that it really mattered, not with our wager anyway.

If it snowed, I took him to dinner. If it didn't snow, he took me to dinner.

Assuming, of course, that he got back to Houston before he had to leave again.

I didn't come right out and ask Mrs. Miller how long he was planning to stay here. I figured she wouldn't know anyway.

James didn't seem like the kind of guy who shared that kind of information even if he had it. Which I didn't think he did.

He might have a general idea how long he planned to stay, but if he was called back for a flight, he would leave early.

I knew how it went.

Pilots were all about the love of the flight.

Standing outside in the freezing cold, waiting for the dogs to do their business, I watched the traffic.

The cold weather might have kept me at home, but the buses were still running and it looked like most people were still out for morning rush hour.

Schools were always one of the first things to close when there was bad weather.

A small jet flew past overhead, sending my heart into a summersault.

It wasn't James, but for just that brief instant, I thought maybe it could be.

And what's more, I thought maybe I wanted it to be.

I definitely wanted it to be him.

There was something about him. I couldn't stop thinking out him.

Handsome. Kind. Smart. What was not to like?

"How is Mrs. Miller?" Jose asked as he opened the door for me to go back inside.

Even the puppies were looking a little cold. They might be huskies, but they weren't used to the cold weather.

"She seems good. How are you?"

"I'm good. My kids are home today. They are still hoping for snow, but I don't know. I am afraid they will be disappointed."

"They closed the college, too," I said. "Seems like they just wanted to get our hopes up that we were going to get snow."

"Ah," Jose said. "They try to mess with our heads. Make us think we're going to have a white Christmas."

"I think you're right," I said.

Jose pushed the elevator button.

"Have a good day, Dr. Devereaux," he said.

"You too, Jose."

As I rode up the elevator with the puppies, I wondered why he had called me Dr. Devereaux. He'd always just called me Miss Genevieve.

The concierge probably said something to him. I shrugged it off and stepped off the elevator.

The puppies ran ahead, stopping right in front of Mrs. Miller's door.

"You're smart dogs, aren't you?" I asked them.

Holly barked once. Molly just sat and looked at me with big puppy dog eyes while I opened the door.

They dashed inside and raced to the back where Mrs. Miller waited.

Glancing at the clock, noting that I had slept too late, I left, closing the door behind me.

As I walked across the hall, the elevator doors opened and James stepped off.

I froze right there at my door, one hand on my doorknob.

"Hi," he said, walking toward me.

"Hi. How are you here? I thought the airport was closed."

"It is," he said. "I didn't use the airport."

There was no way he had driven from Dallas.

The roads in Dallas were closed for snow. I had checked.

It was almost like I had wished him here and here he was.

"I don't understand," I said.

"I have a date with a beautiful woman," he said. "A man will do just about anything to make sure he doesn't miss that."

Chapter Sixteen

James

When I got off the elevator of the twenty-fifth floor, the very person I had hurried back to see was standing right there.

Sometimes, it seemed, fate intervened.

Genevieve was just as beautiful as I had remembered. Maybe more so.

I had a good memory but her big green eyes framed by thick lashes... her smooth looking skin... and her full bow-shaped lips... altogether made her look like a goddess. A goddess I had trouble taking my eyes off of.

She looked a little bit different today. No makeup. And her hair was pulled back in a messy ponytail.

She was absolutely adorable.

"I know there's more to this story than that," she said.

I grinned. Beautiful and smart. Nothing got past her.

"You might be right," I said.

"Do you want some hot chocolate?" she asked, nodding in the direction of her door. "You can tell me all about this magical transportation device you have."

"Okay," I said. "You twisted my arm."

We stepped inside her condo. It was quickly becoming a familiar place. A place I felt comfortable. The only thing a little odd was that there were no Christmas decorations.

She filled the electric tea kettle with water and turned it on.

"Let me guess," she said. "You didn't actually make it to Dallas."

"Oh no. I made it to Dallas."

She looked at me with obvious suspicion.

I pulled out my phone and held up a picture I had taken of the Phenom. In the snow.

It was the same picture I had sent to Noah Worthington. Just before they took it into the hangar.

Genevieve glanced at it as she placed tea bags in the two mugs.

"Okay," she said. "I saw pictures like that one the weather channel."

And, of course, she wasn't sure whether she believed me or not. It did seem rather fishy.

"Unfortunately I didn't think to take a selfie."

"It's okay," she said, pouring water into a mug and sliding it over to me. "I believe you. It's just curious."

She filled a second mug with hot water and we walked over to sit on her sofa.

"Your university closed today?" I asked.

"They closed for cold weather." She glanced out the window. "And a slight possibility of snow."

"They have to be safe," I said.

She inhaled the warm steam from her mug.

"So tell me about your magical underground tunnel connecting Dallas and Houston."

"Someone has a good imagination."

"I read fantasy," she said. "And Houston actually has an underground system of tunnels downtown."

"I know. But they don't go all the way to Dallas."

"Okay. So not tunnels," she said. "Some other kind of portal."

"Only if you count air travel."

"They let you fly?"

"Yes. But not an airplane."

She took a sip of tea and looked at me over the rim.

"I'm a bit baffled."

"Rightly so," I said. "I travelled by helicopter."

"Ah," she said. "Helicopter. How did you manage that?"

"I actually have a helicopter license."

"You fly helicopters? I thought you were an airplane pilot."

"I can do both."

The train passed by below, blowing its horn at the intersection.

"I've never known a helicopter pilot."

"Well," I said. "You can now say that you do."

"Where did you land?" she asked. "At the airport?"

"I could have, but there's a building across the street with a helipad. I walked from there."

"I'm impressed."

"Then my training was worth every minute."

She made a little face, but what she didn't know was that I was serious.

Chapter Seventeen

Genevieve

James was wearing his pilot's uniform this morning.

Black pants and a black blazer with a white button-down shirt.

Clean-shaven, he looked like a model. Or a pilot. Sometimes it was hard to tell.

My younger brother liked to joke around that pilots and models were interchangeable. Sometimes I almost believed him.

I couldn't imagine the level of skill and knowledge required to fly both airplanes and helicopters.

Not to mention the time and effort that went into all of it.

"You're an anomaly," I said.

"There's a compliment in there somewhere," he said, but a smile played about the corner of his lips.

"Nothing but compliments," I said. "Do you ever get them mixed up?"

"No," he said. "It's like flying a Cessna and a Phenom."

"Just different airplanes."

"Yes. Different airplanes. It's like flying different airplanes."

"I can't even imagine."

"Do you want to go up in an airplane or a helicopter first?"

"Oh. I've been up in airplane," I said, maybe a little too dismissively.

"Oh?"

"We have three pilots in the family."

He looked confused for a moment, then realization flickered over his features.

"You're part of *that* Devereaux family."

I smiled. "Yes. That Devereaux family. They all work for Skye Travels."

"I'm a Skye Travels man, myself."

"Your mother didn't mention that."

He shrugged. "She probably didn't even think about it."

"She certainly didn't tell me you fly helicopters."

"I don't talk about it much," he said.

"Why not? It's an awesome ability."

"It was always just something I did for fun."

"You should tell people," I said.

"I'm probably going to be talking about it more now," he said.

"Oh? Why is that?"

"I had a meeting yesterday with Noah Worthington."

"The man himself."

James smiled. "He is rather impressive. Anyway, he found out that I fly helicopters."

"And?"

"He wants to add some helicopters to his fleet."

"No way. He wants you to fly them."

"Well. He wants to buy one. He wants me to be his first helicopter pilot. Sort of a pilot program."

"Since you're already licensed and you work for him, it's low risk."

"You sound like him."

"I come from a Skye Travels family."

"Frightening."

"Are you going to do it? Fly his helicopter?"

"I don't know yet," he said. "It comes with a catch."

"Besides more money?"

"Yeah," he said with a little laugh. "Besides that."

"What's the catch?"

"It's a big one. It requires relocation. To Houston."

"Oh." An odd little tingle ran along my spine.

I reverted to my psychological training to compensate for the strong emotions that ran through me.

"How do you feel about that?"

Chapter Eighteen

James

It hadn't even occurred to me until that moment that I was sitting with a psychologist.

"How do you feel about that?" Genevieve asked, hiding her expression behind her mug.

"I don't know yet," I said. "It's a major deal."

The truth was that I was not exactly objective about it at the moment.

When Noah had told me about his proposition, the first thing I had thought about wasn't how I would have to uproot myself and move back from Pittsburgh. Or leaving my friends, including the girl I was sort of non-exclusively seeing, behind. It hadn't been coming back to the brutal summer weather which was one reason I had been okay with leaving Houston to begin with.

It had been Genevieve.

I only just met her three days ago.

I wasn't supposed to be making life decisions based on my feelings for a girl I had just met three days ago.

A girl I had not even gone on a date with yet. Even if that was about to change, probably tonight if I had anything to do with it.

"You're from Houston, right?" she asked.

"The Woodlands, yes."

"Then it shouldn't be all that much of a hardship for you. Coming back to your roots and all."

"Are you trying to sway me toward taking the job, Dr. Devereaux?"

"Just an observation. A psychologist never imposes their opinions on a client."

"Good thing I'm not a client."

"Ha. You're not kidding."

Our gazes locked. I looked into her green eyes. Eyes that a man could tumble right over into and never want to come out of.

Definitely not objective.

I hadn't been objective about it from the get go.

Noah may as well have just told me that I was moving back to Houston. It would have saved everyone a lot of time if he'd just told me instead of asking.

The funny thing was if he had asked me just one day—just one day—earlier I might—just might have said no.

No there was no way for me to know which way I would have gone.

Genevieve was like a siren calling me across the rocks with her big green eyes. I was helpless against the lure of her beauty.

"Would you like some more hot chocolate?" she asked.

I glanced at my watch.

"Actually. Would you like to get some lunch?"

"Lunch? I have some work I need to get done."

"Isn't this a free day for you?"

"Psychologists don't get free days."

"No. Well. That's just sad. But you have to eat, right?"

She closed her eyes for just a moment.

"You're very persuasive."

"Am I? That's good to know."

"And you might be a little bit incorrigible."

"Now you're just trying to compliment me."

"Has anyone ever been able to refuse your charm?" she asked.

"I'm charming?"

"Okay," she said, standing up. "Let's go get some lunch."

Chapter Nineteen

GENEVIEVE

I took my time getting ready.

It was only a little after eleven and James was waiting at his mother's so I really didn't have to hurry.

Still. Taking my time was my own little form of rebellion.

James was too dangerous.

He may or may not be moving back to Houston.

The possibility that he might be moving back to Houston gave me hope. I had, however, to temper that hope with the reality that he and I had never even been on a date.

I barely knew him.

And, I had to keep reminding myself, knowing his mother wasn't the same as knowing him. Just because she talked about him all the time didn't mean that I knew him. There were things she hadn't told me. Like him being a helicopter pilot. She might not even know that. There would be a lot of things she didn't know about him and even more things that she hadn't told me about him.

I put on a pair of jeans and a sweater. Some low ankle boots. Then took a few minutes to add some loose curls to my hair.

It wasn't anything more than I would do if I was going to lunch with my own brother, or so I told myself.

The tremble in my fingers, on the other hand, was quite a bit different.

I smeared on some lip gloss and declared myself ready.

James was waiting for me in the hallway. He'd changed, too, out of his uniform and was wearing a long black wool coat and gloves.

When he smiled and straightened from where he had been leaning against the wall, my heart melted.

I felt a little bad, now, for making him wait, but he didn't seem to mind.

"What are the puppies doing?" I asked.

"Curled up in the bed with my mother."

"I don't know a lot about broken bones, but I thought she'd be up more by now and moving around."

"She has physical therapy in the morning. I'll find out what she's supposed to be doing."

Knowing that he would still be here tomorrow sent a smile to my lips. I had wondered if we were going to lunch in lieu of dinner.

It was good to know that he wasn't leaving today. Of course, with the weather, it was hard to say.

Christmas music spilled from speakers in the lobby and the twinkling Christmas trees had me rethinking again about not having a tree of my own.

"You don't decorate for Christmas?" James asked.

"No. I'm going to be spending my two-week Christmas break with my family. Since I won't be home for Christmas, there didn't seem to be much point in it."

"Except that you could be enjoying it now."

"There is that. But I'm leaving next Friday, so it's a little late."

The doorman opened the front door and we stepped outside.

"Did you call for your car?" I asked.

"Actually. No." He unlocked his phone. "I'm calling for an Uber."

"You don't have to do that," I said. "We can take my car." I looked around for Jose. He would go get my car from the parking garage.

"There's an Uber nearby," he said. "Five minutes."

I shrugged. "Okay."

"You know what?" he said. "Why don't we walk? I hear the restaurants behind us are good."

I shivered from the cold.

"Okay," I said. "Let's walk."

He put his phone away and we hit the sidewalk leading around the building to the shopping and restaurant area behind the building.

Called Uptown Boulevard, it was decorated in sparkly gold trees and tinsel and clear lights draped overhead from one side of the little street to the other.

Christmas music spilled from the different shops giving it a small town feel.

"Good choice," I said. "It's all festive."

"Ah. So you do like Christmas."

"I never said I didn't like Christmas."

We walked past a real blue spruce tree one of the shop owners had set up just outside their door. Its clean scent perfumed the air.

The shop owner, a middle-aged woman came out carrying a box of decorations.

"No. You just haven't bothered to decorate."

"If you must know, I helped your mother decorate."

'I didn't know that."

"There are a lot of things we don't know."

There were a lot of things I didn't know about him, but I wanted to know everything.

We stepped out of the cold into a little French bistro.

Oddly enough, I'd never even been here. It was just steps from my door and I had never been here.

James just might be a good influence.

Even if he didn't decide to stay in Houston, though I couldn't imagine why he wouldn't, he was already a good influence.

Chapter Twenty

James

After lunch, we walked along the shopping area sidewalks. Christmas music spilled from the different shops and some of the shops had decorated or were in the process of decorating the areas outside their respective doors.

My phone chimed with a text.

"I just need to check this," I said, pulling my phone from my pocket. "Could be work."

"Sure. Go ahead."

"Oh." I frowned at the screen.

"Something wrong?"

"What? No. Just..."

I put my phone away without answering.

The texts, two of them, were from Angela.

. . .

ANGELA

I called your office. They said you were in Houston with your mother. I hope everything is okay.

ANGELA

Let me know if you need anything. I'm just a short flight away.

I hadn't called Angela. Now I was going to have to.

Genevieve was looking at me with a questioning expression.

"It's just... nothing."

I realized something about myself in that moment. Something that I really hadn't thought much about because it hadn't come up/

I was not one of those guys who could comfortably play the field, dating more than one girl at the time. I was most definitely a one girl at the time kind of guy.

And knowing that I was about to uproot my life to come to Houston, Genevieve was the logical choice.

It wasn't just that she was here, although that was part of it. It would have been her either way.

I had to talk to Angela. I needed to talk to her, but it was one of those conversations that needed to be face to face. I'd talk to her when I got back to Pittsburgh.

"Here we go," I said, jumping on the first diversion that came to my attention.

"Here we go what?" she asked.

I pushed open the nearest shop door and we stepped inside.

It looked like Christmas threw up all over it.

"It's a Christmas shop," she said.

And it smelled like Christmas, too. Like spruce and cinnamon and vanilla.

"I know. What do you think? What should we get you?"

"I don't need anything," she said.

"You do. You need..." I picked up a red mug. "You need Christmas mugs. Two of them."

She smiled. "Yes. Maybe I do."

"Do you like the red or the green?"

"The red."

I took two of them and we walked toward the checkout counter. There were two people ahead of us.

While we waited, Genevieve looked around. She stopped to pick up a snow globe. It had a little couple inside, kissing.

She shook it and watched the glittering snow falling around them.

The line moved and it was our turn to check out.

She set the snow glove down and joined me at the counter.

Now I knew exactly what to get her for Christmas.

As we left the shop, a shimmering little shopping bag in my hands, I smiled over at Genevieve.

It was telling, to me, that I had an idea what to get Genevieve for Christmas but I hadn't thought about getting anything for Angela, the girl I'd been spending time with.

Chapter Twenty-One

Back in our building, we rode up to the twenty-fifth floor.

"Here you go," James said, handing me the shimmering shopping bag. "You now have something Christmassy for your home."

I took the bag from him.

"Yes I do."

"You have work to do and I have puppies to take for a walk."

"Right," I said, standing outside my door.

He was right. I did have work to do. I didn't, however, want to do it so much right now.

That was the problem with taking time off from work. Taking time off led to wanting to take more time off.

It was like spending time with James. Spending time with James led to wanting to spend more time with him.

He started to walk toward his mother's door, then stopped and turned around.

"Do you want to go to dinner tonight?"

"It could still snow. Are you sure you don't want to give it another day?"

"Maybe. This could be separate from our wager."

"Oh. Like a... date?"

"Yes. Very much like a date. Not just like a date, but a date."

I smiled.

"I would like that."

"Perfect. We'll take my mother's car."

"I don't know what she drives, but okay."

"I'll come and get you at seven?"

"Sure," I said, unlocking my door. "See you at seven."

I went inside and closed my door.

Looking at my home from a different perspective, I could see what he meant. It did need some Christmas cheer.

I took off my coat and hung it in the coat closet. Then, taking my little shopping bag to the kitchen, I unwrapped the mugs and washed them.

They looked a little out of place, being the only Christmassy thing in my condo.

It was okay though. I decided to try one of them out.

I heated some water and made some hot tea.

Then I took my new Christmassy mug with me to my desk and got to work.

My attention only strayed occasionally as I tried to focus on making a PowerPoint for an upcoming lecture.

As I worked, my thoughts worked out some possibilities of what I would wear on my first date in forever.

Finally, about mid-afternoon when I took a break to listen to the neighbor playing Christmas music on their piano, I went to stand at my closet.

I didn't even know where we were going.

Wherever it was, I was pretty sure it wasn't a casual dinner. I needed to wear something nice. Something that would look good no matter where we went.

I'd bought a dress for the psychology department's holiday party next week. It was a green velvet dress that was most definitely Christmassy.

That, I decided, was what I would wear.

It was perfect if for no other reason than James wouldn't be able to accuse me of not liking Christmas any more.

Only someone who liked Christmas would wear a dress like this.

It was too early to get dressed, so I went to my reading chair and read the next chapter in the fantasy novel I was reading.

It was hard to focus and not watch the clock, knowing I had a date tonight. A date with someone I actually liked.

When my sister, Anastasia, called on Face Time, I realized I was supposed to have called her back already.

"Are you okay?" she asked. "No one has heard from you lately."

"I'm fine. I've just been busy."

"Understandable." She poured the contents of two measuring cups into a mixing bowl.

I took a sip from my mug.

"What are you doing?" I asked.

"I'm making my gingerbread cookies."

"Not fair," I said.

"Not my fault you're not here. Wait," she said. "What's that?"

"What's what?"

"That mug. You actually have something Christmassy?"

"Why wouldn't I?"

"It's not that you wouldn't," she said. "It's that you don't."

"Well," I said. "I do now."

"Yes. I see that you do."

With a little shrug, I set it down.

"Wait," Anastasia said.

"What?"

"What's that little secret smile about?"

"What smile?"

"Genevieve, do you have a boyfriend?"

"I do not," I said indignantly.

Anastasia narrowed her eyes at me as she stirred the cookie mix.

"Where did you get the mug?"

"I... the neighbor."

"The one with the puppies?" she asked.

"Yes. Her son." I winced as soon as I realized what I had just told her.

"Is he good looking?"

"Not bad," I said, unable to hold back the little smile that played about my lips.

"When do we get to meet him?"

"It's not like that."

"Where are you going tonight?"

"Dinner," I said. "Wait. How did you know?"

Anastasia tapped her temple. "I used my keen detective skills. You didn't go into work today. And. You fixed your hair."

"Maybe I had a Zoom call," I said.

"Maybe. But not on Wednesday. You, my dear sister, are a creature of habit."

"I guess I am."

She wasn't wrong. I did have a rather orderly life and I liked it that way.

James, however, was not an orderly life kind of guy.

He was the kind of guy who could turn a girl's life upside down.

A girl could tell these things.

Chapter Twenty-Two

James

One of the good things, the many good things, about being a pilot was that I always had a formal suit with me.

By the nature of our business, we attended a lot of formal affairs. Galas. Fund raisers. Weddings.

As pilots, we weren't the billionaires, but we were pilots for the billionaires.

And these billionaires often took us as guests wherever they went.

As such I was always prepared.

Tonight might be just dinner, but I showered and donned my suit.

Because it wasn't just dinner. It was a date with Genevieve Devereaux.

And I was not bringing her flowers.

I had a better idea.

I should get points for being nothing if not imaginative.

After running a brush through my hair, adjusting my tie, and telling Mother goodnight, I went across the hallway.

I was feeling rather proud of myself as I waited for Genevieve to answer the door.

But one look at her and I forgot everything except how stunningly beautiful she was.

Her hair fell over her shoulders in loose curls and her lips shimmered with sparkly gloss.

She wore an emerald green velvet dress that hugged her waist with a darker green sash that fell to one side.

"You look beautiful," I said.

"You look handsome yourself."

"Want to come in while I get my—" She stopped in midsentence as she noticed something behind me. "What is that?"

"Oh. Right. In lieu of flowers, I brought you something else you might like."

She returned her gaze to mine, with her sparkling green eyes.

"You brought me a tree."

"Yes," I said, reaching down and lifting up the trunk. "Permission to bring it inside?"

"Yes," she said, opening the door wide. "Please do."

I dragged the seven-foot live blue spruce still wrapped in twine through her door.

"Where to?" I asked.

"Just 'um. Here." She gestured to the living room. "I don't have a stand or lights or any kind of decorations."

"I was thinking that would be tomorrow's date."

"Oh. Well. You think ahead."

"I guess it's a hazard of the trade. Kind of have to have everything mapped out before you take an airplane in the air."

"I guess you do."

My phone chimed with a text message.

"Sorry about that," I said, "I'll just turn it off."

I pulled out my phone and before I could turn off the volume, I noticed I had another text from Angela.

I was definitely going to have to have a conversation with her sooner rather than later.

"Anything important?" Genevieve asked.

"No." I shook my head. "Just a thing. I'll take care of it later."

"Okay." Genevieve smiled and nothing else mattered.

Chapter Twenty-Three

James was full of surprises tonight.

First, instead of flowers, he brought me a tree.

A tree and the promise of a date tomorrow to decorate it.

No one had ever brought me a real tree and I'd actually never even heard of anyone getting a seven-foot Christmas tree wrapped in twine in lieu of flowers.

He had noticed that I hadn't decorated for Christmas and he had brought me a tree to decorate.

I was charmed.

Second, instead of taking his mother's car, he had a car with a chauffeur waiting.

I knew that it was standard for pilots to have drivers when they had premier clients.

But since I was not a client, much less a premier client, it was quite unexpected.

"Noah Worthington is trying to lure me back to Houston," he offered as an explanation.

"It's a little unusual for a current employee to have his boss wooing him for what is essentially a promotion, isn't it?"

"I suppose it is. He wants me here."

"Is it working?" I asked with a little smile.

"Not by anything he's doing," James said, leaving me wondering.

He had reservations at an Italian restaurant where we were seated at a secluded little table.

A red rose lay across an empty plate where I sat down.

I picked it up and inhaled the sweet scent.

"You did this?" I asked.

"I didn't forget to bring you a flower," he said.

"It's a lovely touch," I said. "Thank you."

"You're welcome."

The server brought bottle of champagne and filled our flutes.

"To chance," James said, holding up his glass.

"To chance."

I tapped my glass to his.

"Everything," I said. "Tonight is so unexpected."

"Just a little something I threw together."

"I would be afraid to see something you labored over."

He grinned.

"Speaking of laboring, did you get a lot of work done today?"

"I did. Not that I will ever get it all done."

"The life of a college professor is not as easy as people think."

"You say that like you have some experience in it."

"My sister was a professor before she became a mother. She worked harder than anyone I've ever known."

"You mother told me she's an accountant."

"She is now. Part time. She taught accounting. I think she still teaches adjunct, too."

"Well. If the accounting class I took in college is any indication, accounting is not something I would want to tangle with."

"My sister's good at it. She loves it."

"Your mother should be very proud. She has two very successful children."

"Yours too," he said. "Three pilots and a psychologist."

"Not to mention a little brother who's still in college. Not sure what direction he'll go."

"There are five of you."

"Yep. A big family."

"I'm in awe."

I took a sip of my champagne.

"I wouldn't have it any other way."

"You want a big family of your own?"

"Of course I do. It's what I know."

He gave me a rather quizzical look, one that seemed to hold a lot of questions.

I was rather relieved that the server came to our table then to take our order and I didn't have to answer any of what I had a feeling were hard questions.

I wanted to simply enjoy the evening.

I was with the most handsome man here at a nice restaurant.

That was all I wanted to think about right now.

I didn't want to think about my past or even an uncertain future.

Right now was enough.

Chapter Twenty-Four

I was with the most beautiful girl here in a little Italian restaurant that had come highly recommended by Noah Worthington himself.

When I'd inquired about a nice place to take a girl to dinner, he had given me three recommendations and tossed in a car with a chauffeur.

I'd asked him if the car and chauffeur came with the job.

He had simply responded that "anything is negotiable."

Between Noah sweetening the deal at every turn and Genevieve, I knew I might as well start packing up my house in Pittsburgh.

Angela was still texting me. I had to take care of that situation. She had gotten too attached while I hadn't. I liked her and I enjoyed her company, but I'd never considered taking the relationship to the next level.

But she didn't light up my world like Genevieve did.

Genevieve had been it from the moment I'd seen her.

After dinner, we headed back to her building.

The lights of the Post Oak Boulevard Christmas trees danced on both sides of the street as we traveled. The driver had tuned into the radio station that played music that synced to the tree lights.

I felt a little pang at the thought of giving up my view of the three rivers in Pittsburgh.

The Ohio. The Alleghany. The Monongahela.

A picturesque city perched among the hills with hundreds of bridges over the three rivers.

I had never thought I would live there forever, of course. I was a Texan, born and bred and Houston was my home.

It wasn't like moving back would be a hardship.

Especially not with Genevieve here. Noah might be trying to lure me back, but the truth was, he wasn't the one doing it. She was.

She was luring me back one glance... one smile... at the time.

I didn't stand a chance.

I reached over took her hand.

She carried the rose I'd arranged to have waiting for her at our table.

I was finding it a pleasure to do little things for her.

When we pulled up at the front of the high rise, three valets came to open our car doors for us.

My parents had done well when they had chosen this for my mother's home.

At the time, I hadn't wanted to be part of it, not because I cared if they sold the house we'd grown up in, but I hadn't wanted to deal with my father being sick.

The house. The condo. My father's illness. Were all wrapped up into one big thing I hadn't wanted anything to do with.

But now, being here, I was starting to see it differently.

My mother had made a home for herself here. She had made friends.

It was nice that it just so happened that one of those friends was a beautiful goddess named Genevieve.

After we climbed out of the car, I took her hand and we went inside.

It was cold. About thirty degrees by all accounts.

I still maintained that it was going to snow. If it could hold off until Christmas Eve, then all the better.

I personally didn't think the snow was going to be able to hold off that long. Less than two weeks, but my best guess was that snow would be falling by this weekend.

"We have to bring the puppies down for their walk," Genevieve said as we stepped onto the elevator.

"Actually we don't. Not tonight."

"Why not?" She looked at me curiously.

"I hired a dog walker for the evening."

"You did not."

"I did."

The elevator doors opened and we stepped off onto the twenty-fifth floor.

"I thought we could both use the break."

"Is that so?"

"Do you mind?" I asked. I'd been hesitant to hire a dog walker. I'd thought I would ease into it by hiring one for tonight.

"No," she said. "I don't mind. But I don't mind walking them either."

"They're good little dogs, aren't they?"

"They very sweet little dogs."

"It's funny. My mother having a house full of pets when we weren't allowed to have pets growing up."

"Yeah. We didn't have pets either. It's too bad. I think children should have pets."

"Agreed."

We reached her door.

"So," she said. "If you'd like some hot chocolate, I just got two new festive coffee mugs."

"Did you now?"

"Yes. I did."

"In that case, it would be rude to not try them out."

"We don't allow rudeness on the twenty-fifth floor. Only the best hospitality."

"You're doing an excellent job doing just that."

We stepped inside her condo. The tree was going to make it festive befitting the season.

Even without the tree, it was cozy. It wasn't the place so much, of course, as it was Genevieve.

Houston was looking more and more like the best option by the minute.

Chapter Twenty-Five

Genevieve

James and I sat at my kitchen table drinking hot chocolate out of my new red mugs and looked at photos of decorated Christmas trees on the Internet.

The neighbor played classical Christmas music on the piano. Drifting through the windows, it sounded like a distant music box. Soft and heartwarming.

"We seem to agree on style of décor," James said as I took a screenshot of a tree decorated all in red. Red lights. Red ornaments. An angel wearing a red velvet gown at the very top.

"Monochrome," I said. "It goes along with our minimalist tendencies."

"Uh huh. What time do you want to get started tomorrow?"

I warmed my hands on the mug.

"I'm flexible. I'll be here all day. Working on putting together a final exam."

"One of the joys of being a professor."

"One of many," I said. "I have a virtual session with a client, but not until three o'clock."

"How about ten? We can go to the Container Store, then grab some lunch, and come back to get started."

"Sure. Okay."

"I can run home while you're seeing your client. Then we can finish up. Maybe order some pizza."

"And just like that, you planned our whole day."

"I did, didn't I?" he admitted sheepishly. "I would say it's my superpower, but I don't know how not to do it."

"Like me and mnemonics."

"Exactly."

"I think that's sort of the definition of a superpower. Something that just comes naturally."

I clicked to the next page, finding pictures of trees decorated all in silver. It was hard to say which one would look better.

"I guess we'll see what they have and choose a color based on that."

"Do you mind?" he asked. "That I'm a planner?"

I turned and looked into his magnetic soft blue eyes. I was having a bit of trouble finding fault with anything about him. That might be something of a problem in and of itself.

"I'll let you know if I do," I said.

"Deal," he said. "The puppies are back."

"I hear them."

They were in the hallway, barking.

"I need to see if she needs help getting them inside," he said, standing up.

"Okay. It's getting late. And I have an early date in the morning."

He stopped, his hands on the back of the chair, and looked at me with a little smile.

I smiled back and he bent down. Kissed me lightly on the forehead.

"Until tomorrow then," he said. "At ten."

After he went into the hallway, after I heard Mrs. Miller's door close, I picked up our mugs and took them into the kitchen to wash them. I had a dishwasher, but I didn't use it. Since it was just me I used the same dishes over and over.

I'd had a wonderful evening with a charming guy who just might be moving to Houston.

And not only that, he had our day planned out for tomorrow.

It was fortunate that I had a flexible schedule. Apparently his schedule was open, too.

I dried the mugs with a dish cloth and put them back in the cabinet.

If James was moving back to Houston, he had a lot of things to do in Pittsburgh.

Moving across country was an ordeal, especially in December.

I guess we'd see how things went from here. He hadn't even committed to moving, much less when. Somehow we had managed not to talk about the details of his offer.

I went over. Locked my door. And went to get ready for bed.

I really did have an early morning. Unlike today, there would be no sleeping in.

Before James got here, hopefully, I'd have time to finish up the test I was making. Two down. One to go.

James was something of a bad influence in pulling me away from my work.

Maybe that wasn't such a bad thing.

Thinking about his soft blue eyes and his easy smile, I sighed.

Chapter Twenty-Six

James

"We bought a lot of stuff," Genevieve said as the valet left her condo, taking the rolling cart with him. We could have brought it up, but it did look like a lot.

I rubbed my hands together in anticipation of getting her tree decorated.

"We have a lot of work to do," I said.

"I think you're enjoying this a little too much."

I started sorting items, taking them out of their festively decorated glossy bags. Lights. Ornaments. A tree stand and a tree skirt.

We'd hit Target after lunch. There had been so many people around the holiday aisles, it had been hard to navigate. We weren't the only ones who waited to, what was essentially considering when the holiday started, the last minute.

There hadn't been much left, but we'd gotten lucky and found everything we needed between the two stores.

"What's not to enjoy?" I asked, sitting back on my heels. "I'm spending time with a beautiful girl during the best time of year." I grinned at her. "We've got a tree to decorate."

"Yes we do." She smiled back, then pulled the tree stand out of the package. Worked with it a bit.

"You look like you know what you're doing," I said.

"You have to remember. I'm from a small town. We had a real tree every year."

"It's a little hard to picture you there. You seem so at home here in the city."

"Well. My grandmother had a place in Houston. I spent some time with her here."

"I see. That explains a lot."

"You ready to get this tree standing?"

"Sure," she said, standing up, bringing the tree stand with her. "I'm thinking... right here?" She stood at the corner near the windows looking at me over her shoulder.

"I don't think there's a wrong place to put it."

"Since there's an outlet here," she said, setting the stand on the floor.

"Pretty and practical," I said, picking up the tree and carrying it over to the stand. "I'll hold it if you'll fasten the levers."

"Right. You would give me the hard part."

"Okay. You can hold it," I said, but she was already on her knees, tightening the levers on the stand.

"Almost there," she said.

"How did you do that so fast?" I asked, carefully testing to make sure the tree was held tight and steady. It was.

"I measured." Genevieve stood up.

"How?" She had nothing to measure with on her.

I took a step closer to her.

"I can't tell you everything," she said softly, looking at me with her big green eyes.

I took her hand. Kissed the back of her fingers.

I wanted to kiss her. Should kiss her right... about... now.

"Well," she said. "We have a lot to do."

She slipped out of my hands and went back to sit on the sofa.

"Right," I said, turning back to the tree and turning it just a little so its best side was facing us. It would be easier to tell after it had time to settle.

"You know," I said. "It probably needs a couple of days to—"

"Uh oh."

"What?" I turned around.

She sat on the sofa, frowning.

"What's wrong?"

"I think we forgot something."

"What did we forget?" I asked looking around at all the things surrounding us.

"Hooks," she said. "For the decorations."

"Hooks. Right. I'm sure my mother has some."

"She doesn't. We ran out, too."

"What did you do about it?"

"We hung them directly on the tree limbs in the back where nobody could see."

"We can't do that," I said.

"I know." She glanced at her watch. "I have to get ready for my session."

"Already? Okay. I'll go out and get some while you're in session."

"You may not find any," she said. "I can order them. Have them here tomorrow."

"I'll find some."

"Okay. I'll see you after four o'clock."

I'd find the hooks.

Anything for Genevieve who I was starting to think of as my girl.

Chapter Twenty-Seven

Genevieve

In my training and subsequent work as a psychologist, I had come to believe that it was the little things that tripped up a man, or a woman, as the case may be.

Today cemented that belief in my psyche.

I had finished up with my client and was charting some notes on the session when someone knocked on my door.

That would be James. Back already.

I had to give him credit. If there were hooks to be found, he would find them.

It had been less than two hours and yet it seemed like forever since I'd seen him.

It had been hard not to think about him while I was focused on helping my client. Fortunately I had a lot of experience in focusing. He made it especially hard not to think about how he had almost kissed me.

He would have kissed me, too. I was certain of it. But I hadn't been ready. I'm not sure why. I just wasn't.

When he didn't come inside, I got up to let him in.

With a smile, I opened the door.

But James wasn't on the other side of the door.

It was a tall woman who looked like a model. Her straight blonde hair swept her shoulders in one of those modern haircuts. She literally looked like she'd just had her hair done at a salon.

I shoved self-consciously at my hair. I'd barely even checked it since this morning.

"Hi?" I said.

My first thought was that she must be one of Mrs. Miller's caregivers or maybe one of her therapists. But that didn't fit. This woman wasn't dressed like either.

She wore a dress. A black sequined dress. More like someone would wear out on a date. And with her three inch heels, she towered several inches over me.

"Hello," she said. "I'm sorry to bother you." She motioned over her shoulder. "But Mrs. Miller said I could find James over here. But I think she must be mistaken." She sounded like she looked. Polished. Sophisticated.

"James." I repeated.

"Yes. Her son. He's visiting."

"You're looking for James." I couldn't quite wrap my head around why this woman would be looking for James.

"Yes." She smiled. "It's a surprise."

The elevator came to a stop and the doors opened.

James stepped off and started walking this way. He held a little shopping bag in his hand.

"Oh," the woman said. "There he is. So sorry to bother you."

She turned and walked straight him, throwing her arms around him and kissing him on the lips.

It all happened so fast, I truly thought I was imagining it.

She took his hands and said something to him.

He looked over her shoulder toward me.

There was something in his eyes. Just a flash and then it was gone.

Not able to watch anymore, I closed my door. Locked it.

In a daze, I walked over to my reading chair and sat down.

My mind went blank and I let it.

She was his girlfriend. She'd come here to surprise him.

He'd certainly looked surprised.

He hadn't resisted her. Definitely his girlfriend. He wasn't married. Mrs. Miller would have told me that. But she wouldn't necessarily know if he had a girlfriend.

It was obvious they knew each other well.

I hadn't asked him if he had a girlfriend. I should have asked him.

But the truth was, I hadn't wanted him to have a girlfriend. I had let myself assume that he was single.

I was glad I hadn't kissed him.

And yet... I'd thought we had something. A connection. A true connection.

I had never been so wrong.

Chapter Twenty-Eight

An hour later, I stood in front of my Christmas tree, staring at nothing in particular. It was a really nice tree. A blue spruce. And it smelled like a mountain forest.

It was unusual to find such a good tree this close to Christmas. Back home, he could have gone out and cut one down in the woods, but not here in Houston. In Houston, he'd had to find one for sale.

I was feeling deflated. Somehow James had slipped in under my guards and gotten in my heart.

I'd let my guard down. He'd been so disarmingly charming.

Disarmingly charming.

Too much so.

He'd made me aware of just how much I was missing by not

decorating for Christmas. He had brought me a Christmas tree of all things.

A Christmas tree.

And taken me shopping for decorations.

Disarming.

My living room was strewn with everything Christmas.

All in red. We'd gone with red because it was what the store had the most of.

It could have been... so...

It didn't matter what it could have been.

It was awful.

I took a deep breath.

A really deep breath and let it out slowly.

I assured my clients all the time that this deep breathing technique worked. Practiced it with them even.

Not so much.

My neighbor, the pianist, started playing something Christmassy. I didn't recognize it, but I didn't have to. It was one of those sad songs that tugged at the emotions.

I put a hand over my eyes.

I wanted to cry.

But I'd cry later.

Right now I was going to decorate this tree.

I opened up one of the boxes of lights and pulled out the strand.

I knew how to decorate a tree.

If I ever needed a backup to the psychology gig, I could decorate trees for people.

And walk their dogs.

As I put lights on the tree, I made a decision.

I'd go home.

The only thing I had left to do at the university really was final exams.

I could move my finals online and be done with them. Everybody was doing it.

I had been one of the last hold outs for face to face final exams.

Sometimes it just wasn't worth it. There was no shame in changing my mind.

We had bought clear lights. Sparkly clear lights. So magical.

After I finished up the lights, plugged them into the outlet near the window, I went to my bedroom to pack.

I'd leave in the morning.

The Millers could figure out their own lives.

And they would. They would do just that.

James had a girlfriend.

I did not need to hang around here and run the risk of bumping into them.

I also did not want to be here in case James wanted to talk to me. To give me an excuse.

No excuses necessary. I should never have let my guard down.

I wanted to be as far away from him as I possibly could.

Chapter Twenty-Nine

James

The Next Day

Molly and Holly sat quietly at my heels as I knocked on Genevieve's door.

I'd brought the puppies on purpose with the hope that she wouldn't be able to resist them. They liked her and she seemed to like them.

Yes. They were my shield.

But she wasn't coming to the door.

I'd wanted to see her last night. Should have.

But Angela had gotten my mother involved. It made things more complicated.

The caregiver had let her in and she and my mother had talked while I was out buying ornament hooks.

I didn't have it in me to just heartlessly tell her to leave. To her credit my mother didn't say anything about Genevieve to Angela. It was the caregiver who had pointed Angela across the hall.

I'd let her down easily and compassionately. Relatively compassionately.

She had cried, making me feeling heartless. But I had been resolute.

I had used the excuse of moving back to Houston and I had stood my ground. It was true that I didn't want a long distance relationship. I wouldn't want a long distance relationship even if Genevieve wasn't in the picture.

That's what I told myself anyway. Without Genevieve I don't in all honesty know what I would have done about Angela. Maybe I wouldn't even have changed jobs. Maybe I would have stayed in Pittsburgh and I might have even stayed with Angela for a while longer.

Sometimes it took a catalyst to change the status quo. That included relationships.

Angela was persistent. I had no doubt she was the one who had kept us going.

By the time I had convinced her that we wouldn't be seeing each other anymore, it was too late to knock on Genevieve's door.

I was emotionally drained anyway.

Not that I would go around broadcasting it, especially around the guys, but I wasn't cut out for this kind of life.

I was a one girl kind of guy. Better off married. Marriage would suit me. Definitely.

Not ready to give up, I knocked on Genevieve's door again.

No answer.

I'd come back later.

"Come on, Molly. Come on, Holly." I tugged on their leashes and we walked to the elevator.

I passed Jose on the third floor.

"Hello Mr. James," Jose said. "How did Miss Genevieve like her Christmas tree?"

"She liked it fine," I said. "We just have to finish decorating it."

"Yes," Jose said. "You decorate."

Jose opened the door and held it while the puppies dashed outside in front of me.

It was cloudy and still cold. I was going to win my friendly wager with Genevieve since we hadn't set a deadline on it. I was certain it was going to snow before long.

I checked my phone for messages while I waited near the door.

I still didn't have Genevieve's phone number. I could get it from Mother though if it came to it. I'd rather talk to Genevieve in person. I liked to have my important conversations in person.

And that was exactly, I mused, why I was in this situation.

I had put off talking to Angela and she had shown up here at my mother's.

Molly came running back to stand at my feet, wagging her tail. A few seconds later Holly joined her.

"Ready?" I asked.

Holly barked once.

"Okay then. Let's go."

Jose opened the door and I followed the puppies inside.

"It's a bit cold," I said.

"Mr. James," Jose said. "I need to tell you something."

"What is it Jose?" The puppies went to the ends of their leashes and stopped.

Jose shifted his feet and looked over his shoulder.

"I probably shouldn't tell you, but I don't think you know and I think you should know."

"What is it?"

"Miss Genevieve. She left this morning."

"She left?"

"Yes. I helped her put her luggage in her car."

"Where did she go?"

"She went home, Mr. James. For Christmas."

"Home."

The puppies raced back and I reeled in their leashes to keep them close and out of trouble.

"Somewhere north of the city," Jose said. "I just thought you should know."

Chapter Thirty

GENEVIEVE

I stood in front the Christmas tree in my family's living room.

It was massive compared to my blue spruce and unlike my tree, it was fully decorated.

Multi-colored twinkling lights. Christmas lights in all colors. Ornaments in all colors. I recognized some of the decorations from my childhood. No theme. Just randomly thrown together.

It was all topped off with silver icicles and the angel that had been handed down through the generations secured at the top.

Brightly wrapped gifts—all colors and designs—sat beneath the tree.

It was beautiful.

The house smelled like Christmas. An apple pie in the oven. A fire in the fireplace.

My family started their Christmas celebrations early.

The grandfather clock near the staircase chimed the hour. Six o'clock.

My older brother Austin came in through the back door, his arms loaded down with firewood.

He set it next to the fireplaced and dusted off his hands. Our mother didn't allow for dropping firewood.

Kneeling, he added a couple of logs to the fire and arranged them with the poker, sending sparks up the chimney, a few of them landing on the hearth.

Satisfied, he turned around, his back to the fire.

My brother was older than me by about five years. Newly married. A pilot.

"You're not supposed to be here," he said.

"I know," I said with a little smile.

"You look like you lost your best friend."

There was no way to hide anything from my family. I'd come here for solace and to retreat from James.

They knew I wasn't due to be here for at least another week. I couldn't expect them not to notice that something was bothering me. Of course they would notice. It was what family did.

They knew each other better than anyone.

And my family was close.

"I'll be okay," I said.

"When you get ready to talk about it, I'm here," he said.

Unexpected tears sprang to my eye.

"I know," I said.

"Come here." He scooted closer and gave me a hug.

I rested my cheek against his shoulder and my tears soon dampened his shirt.

"Tell me his name," Austin said. "And say the word. I'll punch out his lights."

He shoved my hair back.

I smiled and bit back a little laugh.

"Somehow I don't think that would be helpful."

"You'd be surprised. But you're right. It would help me more than it would help you."

"I'm glad you realize that."

I straightened and wiped at my eyes with my sleeve.

"When a guy has a psychologist for a sister he tends to pick up things here and there."

I took a deep breath. Let it out slowly.

"Seriously though," he said. "Let me know what I can do."

"I will," I said. "Thank you, Austin."

"Now," he said. "What did you get me for Christmas?"

"I knew there was something I was forgetting to do."

Family. I'd been right to come here.

Being with my family would make everything okay again.

Chapter Thirty-One

JAMES

I walked around the helicopter, doing a visual post-flight inspection.

A Sikorsky. Top of the line. Brand new.

"I'll see you inside," Noah said.

"I'll be there shortly," I said.

It had been a pleasure to fly the brand new helicopter Noah had just bought. I was the first to fly it.

Noah'd had me explain everything as I did it. He would be flying helicopters before long. That was just the way he was. He was qualified to fly every airplane in his fleet from the Cessna to the Phenom to the Lear.

Like the rest of us pilots, flying was in his blood. He just happened to have the resources to do something with it.

Genevieve had unknowingly lured me back to Houston and even if I never saw her again, that wouldn't change.

I was back where I belonged and the offer Noah made me to relocate was irresistible. He was giving me a once in a lifetime opportunity. Took care of the sale of my house and would eventually set me up in a new one. I moved in with my mother until I had time to find something.

To top it all off, I went into the chauffeur queue. It was like icing on the cake. Would have taken the offer without it, but it made the deal even sweeter.

With my post flight check completed, I headed inside the Skye Travels terminal building.

Another pilot, also in a Skye Travels uniform was coming inside and we rode the elevator up together.

"Hey," the pilot said. "You just flew the new helicopter."

"Yes. I'm James Miller."

"Austin. Austin Devereaux."

"Devereaux as in *the* Devereauxs."

"Yes," Austin grinned. "Never heard it put quite like that. Not in a good way anyway."

"Right. It's just I've heard so much about your family. I actually know your sister."

"Oh? Which one?"

"Genevieve."

"How do you known Genevieve?"

We got off the elevator on the second floor and walked toward the back where the offices were.

"My mother lives across the hall from her."

James stopped and looked at me.

"Puppies?"

"My mother has two puppies."

"Hm. You wouldn't happen to know why she went home early, would you?"

Oh no. This was one of those moments that could so easily go sideways. Austin obviously knew something about Genevieve and possibly Angela. He wouldn't know details. Couldn't. But he would have a general idea that I had done something to hurt her. There was no excuse either.

"Unfortunately, I might."

"Anything you want to elaborate on? Man to man?"

I was going to ere on the side of honesty. It had served me well in the past and I saw no reason not to continue it. Besides I had good intentions if that meant anything to him and I hoped it did.

"I've got to meet with Noah right now," I said. "but if you'll let me buy you a beer I'd like to talk to you."

"There's a place across the street, called the Sky House Bar and Restaurant. Meet you there after your meeting?"

"Absolutely."

I was relieved that Austin wasn't one of those guys who thought he had to pummel every guy he thought might have wronged his sister in any way. He seemed like a reasonable man.

And I clung to the possibility that he might could actually help me.

In fact, I felt more hopeful than I had felt in a week.

It was with high spirits that I stepped into Noah's office to finalize the deal on my new contract.

Chapter Thirty-Two

GENEVIEVE

Christmas Eve

It was a family tradition, for as long as I could remember, that my entire family walked down Main Street in Maple Creek on Christmas Eve.

It was a little bit for the shopping, but mostly it was for the magic of the hustle and bustle of the little town on Christmas Eve.

Christmas music spilled from the speakers and some of the shops had their own music playing. Standing in one of the doorways was like standing in a portal of a cacophony of music. The music from inside the shop blended with the music outside the shop. It was like the music playing when an orchestra warmed up for a concert. Everything lovely by itself, blending together in unique strains.

Everything twinkled with colorful lights. Nothing elaborate or modern like the tree lights on Post Oak dancing to music on a radio station. Instead, simple strings of sparkling lights strung along from post to post and outlining every window and door. Even the famous boxes of ivies had nets of twinkling lights tossed over them in what looked like studied chaos.

Everything that didn't move, and some that did, got a light or a ribbon or some type of festive decoration.

All the shops stayed open until six o'clock and none of the merchants seemed to mind working late even on Christmas Eve. It was actually the owners mostly who worked, sending the employees home to be with family and possibly to walk the streets themselves.

We weren't the only family with this tradition. A mother and father holding a little girl's hands between them ducked into the ice cream shop.

Seeing them brought a mist to my eyes. It was silly.

I was going to be an aunt soon. Another thought that sometimes brought tears to my eyes.

I couldn't help thinking that I had somehow missed out.

And every time I thought about what that elusive future might look like, an image of James appeared in my mind.

Ava nudged me and the image of James vanished.

"Want to get ice cream?" she asked.

I forced a smile to my lips.

"Sure," I said.

"Come on, Austin. Let's get ice cream."

Ava wasn't a Devereaux by birth, but she'd been around the

family enough to know our traditions. She knew them as well as any of us.

And getting ice cream on Christmas Eve was one of those traditions.

Ava, Austin, and I stepped into the ice cream shop. It smelled like vanilla, salted caramel, and freshly baked waffle cones.

We sat on red stools at the little white bar and waited for our turn to order.

Upbeat Christmas music filled the room along with sounds of laughter and conversations from other people in the shop.

A Christmas tree stood in one corner, decorated with little ice cream cone ornaments in all colors. The twinkling lights, ribbons, and bow at the top were in a pale blue that brought to mind the chilliness of winter and an elusively snowy Christmas Day.

"What kind do you want?" Ava asked. She was trying to be cheer me up. I knew it as well as she did.

"Chocolate and vanilla swirl," I said, swallowing a lump in my throat. Maybe I'd imagined having James here with me on this Christmas Eve. Who could blame me?

Everything seemed hollow somehow without him here. I wanted to introduce him to my family. My roots.

Austin leaned forward, looking at me around his wife.

"Gen," he said.

I waited for him to say more, but he didn't. I met my brother's gaze.

"Austin?"

"At least get sprinkles and peppermint on it."

I wrinkled my nose at him and barely refrained from rolling my eyes.

But when we ordered a couple of minutes later, I added peppermint and sprinkles to my ice cream.

"Ava," Austin said to get my attention again after we got our ice cream.

"What? I got peppermint," I said, holding it up for him to see. "And sprinkles."

"No," he said, keeping his voice in a loud whisper. "You won't believe who just walked in the door."

My heart did a wild nose dive. James. That was my first thought. I couldn't help it.

But even as my heart thought of James, my head knew that it couldn't be him.

It couldn't be him because Austin didn't know James.

If he knew James and my connection to him, then maybe. But I'd only told him sketchy details. Not enough for him to put anything together. Not even his name.

Still, my hands trembled as I turned and looked toward the door.

At first I didn't see anyone I recognized. Then my gaze snagged on a tall fellow wearing a red flannel shirt.

He looked vaguely familiar.

Then. Recognition.

"Zach?"

I looked back at James.

"Zach?"

"Yes. He runs the hardware store now."

Zach saw James and Ava first. Ava waved and he waved back. Then he saw me.

I saw my own confusion reflected in his gaze.

Zach had grown up nicely. He'd gone from a gangly, cute boy to a lean handsome man.

He smiled and walked over to us.

"Genevieve," he said.

"Zachary."

"It's been a minute."

"More than, I'd say."

Setting my spoon down, I stood up and gave him a quick hug.

"How are you?" I asked.

"I'm good. Merry Christmas."

"Merry Christmas. It's good to see you."

I sat back down. Picked up my bowl of ice cream.

Zach rejoined who I recognized as his sister and a man I didn't recognize. Obviously her husband and they appeared to have a little boy who clung to his mother's legs.

Interesting.

That was all I could think.

"He's cute," Ava said.

"He's old news," I told her. "We dated in high school."

"He appears to be single."

I glanced back over at Zach where he stood in line with his family.

"Maybe," I said, scraping some of the peppermint aside before taking a bite of chocolate ice cream. I couldn't figure out how someone decided that peppermint and chocolate ice cream went together. Maybe I was just a purist when it came to my ice cream.

"Maybe you should go out with him," Ava said.

Out of the corner of my eye, I saw Austin shaking his head.

"Not a good idea," he told his wife.

"Why not?"

"She doesn't need to date Zach," Austin said, barely loud enough for me to hear him.

"But—"

"Ava," Austin said. "I'll tell you later."

I frowned at my brother, then just shrugged. I couldn't remember him not liking Zach, but that was another lifetime ago.

He was right. And it didn't matter anyway.

I lived in Houston. Any romance involving my old boyfriend who still lived in Maple Creek would be doomed from the outset.

Truth was, my emotions were still raw from my dive into crushing big time on James.

It would take me a while to get over him.

I would do it, though, and not by dating an old high school boyfriend.

Going backwards was not something I was in the mood for.

Chapter Thirty-Three

GENEVIEVE

Some of my fondest memories revolved around going in to Maple Creek on Christmas Eve, then everyone scattering after we got home to wrap a few last minute gifts.

These were memories I would cherish forever and I knew it.

I wouldn't give up our family traditions for anything.

I would, however, be pleased to share them with someone.

That someone specifically being James.

My heart was bruised and even though I thought about him all the time, I kept coming back to the imagine of Angela kissing him right there in the hallway outside my condo. When he had been coming to see me. To bring the ornament hooks had doubtless found.

He had a girlfriend. I had simply been the neighbor who took care of his mother. It made sense that he would be nice to me.

It didn't make sense that he would want to kiss me.

Maybe I had imagined that part of it. Maybe it had been me wanting to kiss him.

Maybe I had been projecting my desires onto him.

I rolled out some plain red wrapping paper and cut it just right to fit the novel I'd bought my sister Anastasia.

I already had a gift for her, but I'd seen this book and I'd thought of her. So she got it, too.

It was sweet the way my brother Austin had tried to shield me from going on a date with Zach. He knew how attached I was to the man I had met in Houston even if he didn't know his name.

It hadn't been hard to see it and he was the one I had confided in the most in about James.

I'm not sure why. Maybe he had just been there at the right time.

I finished up wrapping my handful of gifts and loaded them up in my arms to take them downstairs to put under the tree.

There was no one else in the living room. As I tucked my Christmas gifts around the tree just I did every year, I heard my sister and sisters-in-law talking in the kitchen. They were making spaghetti for dinner.

We always had something like spaghetti on Christmas Eve, the night before a day of traditional Christmas food. Ham. Turkey. Dressing.

I sat on my heels in front of the tree, watching the twinkling lights.

My gaze landing on one of the ornaments with my name on it.

Wrapping my fingers around it, I smiled. We'd gotten these when we were kids and painted them ourselves.

Mine was obviously written by a child.

Traditions were everything.

This evening reminded me of why I hadn't decorated my condo.

There had been no need.

My Christmas world was here.

I had no reason to decorate in Houston.

It had been fun picking out the decorations for the ideal magazine-worthy perfect tree. But that wasn't real. This was real.

This old-fashioned, no-color-coordinated-whatsoever tree was what Christmas was all about.

I had to remember that. I had to keep things in perspective.

Even though I would date and have crushes on boys who would come and go, family was always here. Family was what everything revolved around.

"Are you okay?" Austin asked, coming to sit on the corner of the couch next to where I knelt in front of the tree.

"I'm okay. Just thinking how good it is that we can still keep up the family traditions."

"We always will," he said. "No matter what."

My eyes misted over again and I blinked back moisture.

"Do you believe in Christmas magic?" he asked after a couple of minutes.

"I don't know," I said. "I guess so."

"You have to," he said.

Turning around, sitting on the floor, I studied my brother.

"Are you being fanciful?"

He grinned. "Maybe a little. But you didn't answer my question."

"I said I guess so."

"Maybe you should try to do a little more than just guess."

"What's up with you?" I asked. "Are you okay?"

"I'm great. Ava is great. We're great."

"Good," I said. "I'm trying not to be jealous."

"Ava and I are going to have a baby."

"Austin that is so incredibly wonderful." I was so truly happy for my brother, my heart swelled.

"Don't worry," he said. "When the time is right, you'll find your soulmate."

"I don't know," I looked down. "Maybe."

"Anything can happen at Christmas."

I thought about James.

About how he'd bought me Christmas mugs when he noticed I didn't have any.

About how he had brought a Christmas tree to my door. Instead of flowers.

About how much fun we'd had going out shopping for Christmas decorations.

And even more than anything else, I remembered the way he'd looked at me. The feel of his hand in mine.

We'd had something real. I was certain of it.

Even if it had been fleeting, it was real.

"I believe in Christmas magic," I said, but when I looked up, Austin had left.

He'd left me sitting here on the floor, staring at the twinkling Christmas lights.

Thinking about James.

"Well," I said. It was okay. I was only now realizing I'd had a taste of that Christmas magic in the time I'd spent with James and now I knew.

Christmas magic really existed.

And like a snowfall on Christmas, when something that rare happened, it was fleeting.

Anything that wonderful couldn't last.

Chapter Thirty-Four

I woke the next morning in my childhood and teenage bedroom.

Even though it was early, I knew before I brushed off the sleepy and oriented myself that today was a special day.

Christmas.

Today was Christmas.

Laughter drifted up from downstairs.

Someone was already up and about. Probably making break-fast before opening gifts.

They wouldn't start until everyone was there. It was one of those unstated rules that we had.

There was no need to hurry.

I stretched in the bed and rubbed my eyes.

I felt better today, I realized.

Family was healing. Always had been.

After taking my time waking up, I got up and padded into my bathroom.

A good hot shower washed off the last of the sleepy. I lingered, letting my mind wander where it would.

It was good to be home. Surrounded by family.

My found family back in Houston at my condo was important to me, too, but I had to remember that my true family was here in Maple Creek. They were the ones who would always be here for me, though thick and thin.

It had been odd seeing Zach after all these years, but I didn't want to date him.

I had moved on. I wasn't the same cheerleading homecoming court girl I'd been in high school.

I was a career woman now and instead of cheerleading, I helped people navigate through problems in their lives. I *helped* people. And not just by cheering them on.

No. After the holidays, I would go back to my condo in Houston. Get back to work. Teaching. Seeing clients. I had a career to pursue.

James would be gone by then and I wouldn't have to worry about seeing him again.

Even if he stayed in Houston, he rarely visited his mother.

Past behavior was the best predictor of future behavior.

I got dressed. Dried my hair. Straightened it and added some loose curls with my curling iron.

Since there would be photos, I added some makeup. Mascara. Lip gloss.

When I checked my appearance in the full length mirror, I couldn't help but smile.

If my students could see me now, they would laugh their heads off.

It wasn't likely that a student would imagine their professor wearing pajamas on Christmas morning.

But I did. It was something we all did. The whole family wore matching pajamas on Christmas. A new pair every year.

It was one of what I considered our most endearing traditions.

Grandma had started it when she used to bring us all pajamas for Christmas. Pajamas that ended up matching.

Hair and makeup ready for spontaneous Christmas morning photos, wearing my brand-new green flannel pajamas, I headed downstairs to join my family.

Chapter Thirty-Five

After a huge breakfast of homemade croissants and loaded omelets, we all took our lattes and gathered in the living room.

My brother Theodore and I were the only ones not paired off. It didn't seem awkward, though. We were all close. Grandma was on a holiday cruise with a man she had started dating and although she was missed, I was happy for her.

Her absence was a reminder to me that we were fortunate to be able to stay together and celebrate Christmas as a family.

Theodore, being the youngest, took the job of handing out the gifts.

It wouldn't be many more years before we had little ones to do that. Things were changing. In a good way. As they should.

Theodore handed me a little square package in shiny solid red gift wrap. It reminded me of the paper back in my condo. The paper James and I had bought at the Container Store. Thick red shiny foil paper.

I turned it over and over, but there was no name tag on it. How did Theodore even know that it was mine?

A quick glance around told me that it was the only gift wrapped in solid red paper.

"Who is this from?" I asked, but no one heard me. Everyone was laughing and opening their own gifts.

Theodore handed me another gift. A festive shirt-sized gift wrapped in colorful reindeer paper.

I went back to the gift wrapped in red foil paper. Slipping a finger under the edge, I slowly unwrapped the plain white box.

Holding my breath, though I couldn't say why, I opened the box lid and moved the white tissue paper aside.

It was a snow globe. The very same snow globe I had looked at in the Christmas store back in Houston. When I'd been out shopping with James. The one with the kissing couple.

I forced myself to take a breath, but my hands were trembling.

How had this gift ended up here? On Christmas morning? Beneath my family's Christmas tree?

I tried to think of a good explanation, but I just couldn't. No one in my family would give a gift without taking credit for it. They either wrote on the paper directly or stuck a name tag on the gift.

Austin was holding up a new jacket someone had given him when he stopped and looked toward the front window.

I just so happened to snap a photo of him when he looked that way. When I looked at it later, I would see that he didn't look surprised, but actually looked relieved.

At the moment, though, he was the first person to hear whatever it was he heard.

He sat the jacket down in his lap and looked at me.

Picking up my coffee mug and sipping my hot latte, looked around and watched my oldest brother Jonathan and his wife Sophia whispering something to each other. They were so cute together.

Then I heard what Austin had heard.

At first I didn't recognize the sound, quickly getting louder and louder.

Everyone stopped talking and followed Austin's gaze toward the window.

"What is that?" someone asked.

I stared out the window, somehow knowing, but not believing what I was hearing.

Living on the twenty-fifth floor, I was familiar with certain sounds that most people wouldn't be.

I was in the flight path of big airplanes and small airplanes.

And helicopters.

A helicopter was coming toward us.

Helicopters did not have a route in Maple Creek. Certainly did not have a route that included our house.

But when it landed in our front yard, right there on the driveway, I knew it could only be one person.

I only knew one person who flew helicopters.

Setting my coffee mug down, I looked at Austin.

He looked back at me with a little smile, unlike everyone else who just looked confused.

Visitors were supposed to come up the driveway in cars. Not helicopters.

"I think someone's here to see you," he told me.

I shook my head, but I stood up anyway and walked toward the front door.

My face felt heated and I felt not a little bit off-balance.

But Austin insisted.

As I opened the front door and stepped out, I realized I needed my coat.

The air was bitingly cold, whipping against my skin.

I couldn't go out there without my coat.

I turned around to get it, but Ava stood behind me, holding out my coat. I threw it on, not taking the time to button it.

With my coat on now, I stepped outside.

If Austin was wrong...

The motor turned off and the blades slowed.

I started walked forward again as the door opened.

My heart was pounding so hard I thought it might beat right out of my chest.

James stepped out the door and climbed to the ground.

He smiled and looked at me with those eyes. Those eyes that told me everything I needed to know.

We stood in front of each other now. I bit my lip. Tried to remind myself that I was mad at him.

"You're here," I said.

"I had a bet to collect," he said.

"A bet? You flew a helicopter to my driveway for... But it's not snowing."

He put his hands on my elbows and looked up toward the clouds.

I followed his gaze.

"My calculations are usually right on the money."

He was smiling at me again.

"Merry Christmas," he said.

"Merry Christmas. Calculations?"

"Yes."

"Calculations for..."

He looked up again.

"There's no snow in the..." Forecast. I stopped talking.

The first snowflake drifted down softly, silently landing on the sleeve of my wool coat. I stared at it, thinking I must have imagined it.

Then the white fluffy flakes drifted down one after another.

"How did you?" I looked at him, trying to figure out how he had done this.

"The snow?" He shrugged. "Predicting snowfall is my other super power."

"Planning and predicting sort of go together," I said distractedly.

"I guess they do." He pulled me a fraction closer. "Is it too late to change the parameters of our wager?"

"Considering everything, I would say yes. Are you trying to get out of taking me to dinner?"

The snow was falling in earnest now. I blinked as a snowflake landed on my eyelashes.

It was beautiful.

"Considering one is about like the other, but no. How about an addendum?"

"You can't add an addendum to a bet after it's already decided."

He removed the glove from his hand and swept a snowflake off my cheek.

"You're not making things easy for me."

"Okay," I said. "What kind of addendum are you talking about?"

"How about... if it snows I get to kiss you?"

"I think you stacked the decks."

He grinned.

"You know what they say," he said.

"What do they say?" I wanted to hold onto being mad at him. Maybe just a little bit longer, but that anger was slipping right out of my hands. The little bit of anger was quickly being replaced by a feeling of warmth.

"All's fair in love and war."

"Is that still the thinking?" I asked. "Because I haven't heard that in a long—"

He bent down then, cutting off anything else I was going to say, and kissed me right on the lips. Kissed me with lips that were firm and soft. Gentle. Lips that caused my heart to flutter, then set itself right back down, but in at a slightly differently angle. And I knew. I knew I would never be quite the same again. My world was forever altered.

"So you admit you stacked the decks?" I asked softly when he pulled back and looked into my eyes.

"I can't take the credit." He put his palm on my cheek and my eyes fluttered closed again.

When I opened them, he was smiling at me with his sparkling blue eyes.

"No snow machine on the helicopter?"

"No snow machine." He ran his fingers through my hair. "We're in our own little snow globe."

"Snow globe…" I said, biting my lip, remembering the gift I had opened a few minutes ago. The snow globe.

"Genevieve. I'm sorry about what happened. I didn't mean—"

I put my fingers against his lips.

"It's okay," I said. "You're here now and it's Christmas."

"Do you have room for one more in there?" he asked, grinning.

"Well. Since you came all this way I think maybe we can fit you in."

I took his hand and together we walked up the sidewalk toward the front door of my family's house.

Through the magic of Christmas, James was here. On Christmas. With me.

From this day forward, I would always and forever be a believer in the magic of Christmas.

With light fluffy snowflakes falling around us as we walked, we smiled at each other, our gazes locked.

The magic of Christmas was real.

"Are you wearing pajamas?" he asked as we neared the front door.

Epilogue

GENEVIEVE

One Week Later
New Year's Eve

James and I sat curled up together on my couch. Molly and Holly also curled up with us.

It was cold and dreary outside. Not snowing. Just cold and dreary looking with low hanging clouds.

It was so cloudy that we didn't have our usual view of downtown from here today. It was like downtown had just vanished.

"I think you brought Pittsburgh weather with you," I said.

"You'll be wishing I had that ability in about July."

"Maybe even May."

"You're right." He made a face. "I did not miss the heat."

"Nothing to miss."

"I know we decided to stay in," he said. "But what do you usually do on New Year's Eve?"

"I'm usually at home with my family, but I usually like to take some time to plan my next year."

"Yeah? Like goals and such?"

"Yes. Goals. Sort of like a vision plan for the upcoming year."

"We could do that."

"Or," I said, picking up the remote to my new television that James had hung on my wall. "Since we have this new television, we could watch a movie."

"We'll do that, too," he said. "But first let's write out our goals. Is that how you do it?"

"Let me get my notebook."

I went to my bedroom and pulled out my goals notebook. I had sort of minimized the importance of this annual activity.

I'd written down my goals and dreams in this same leather notebook every year since I was fifteen. My grandfather had given it to me for Christmas with the suggestion that I use it to write down things that were important to me.

Since the new year was just around the corner I had started it off them. Every year I pulled it out and outlined my goals and dreams for the upcoming year.

Some years I was quite specific and other years I just wrote down some vague ideas. I'd soon noticed that the years following my detailed outlines were usually much more productive.

I flipped to a fresh page and write down the new year at the top.

"You get to go first," I said. "This is your page."

"Yeah? I get to write in what looks like your really nice leather notebook?"

"It is. But I grant you an exception. Only because you bought me a television."

"Okay. I'll go first."

"Let's see. Number one." He wrote clearly and meticulously. "Find a place to live."

"Okay. That's a good goal." Although I knew it was a good goal, I had no enthusiasm for it. Him finding a place of his own meant he would no longer live on the twenty-fifth floor across the hall from me.

And yet I knew he couldn't continue to live with his mother.

Instead of just making a list, he wrote his goals inside little rectangles scattered around the page like a road map.

"You have interesting way of doing this," I said. "I like it."

"It lets me think in priorities."

"Alright. You have one. What's next?"

"I'm actually a fairly simple man."

"I doubt that."

"What? It's okay. You'll see."

I peeked over at his next item.

Get engaged.

I didn't say anything. Just help my breath as he wrote down the next item.

Get married.

He looked up at me, a smile playing about the corner of his lips.

"See? A simple man. That's all I have for the year."

"Those are not exactly what I would call simple goals."

"Seems simple to me."

"I would think that you would have to have certain things in place in order to achieve those goals, especially if you're going to achieve them in the next year."

"I can get a lot done if I set my mind to it," he said.

"I don't doubt that."

"Now we just have to see if our goals align."

"How are we going to do that?" I asked.

Holding out a hand for mine, he pulled me into his lap.

"I was thinking we start with a kiss."

I couldn't disagree. Anytime his lips touched mine, I was lost.

This Christmas had been magical. A magical Christmas sliding right into an equally magical New Year's Eve.

The promise of a lifetime with James would be a lifetime of magic. Enough to take my breath away.

Little flakes of snow swirled around the kissing couple in the little glass snow globe sitting on the coffee table.

It truly was a magical moment.

Keep Reading for a Preview of
Believe in the Magic of Christmas...

AUTHOR OF PERFECTLY MISMATCHED
KATHRYN KALEIGH
Believe in
the Magic of Christmas
THE DEVEREAUXS
BELIEVE IN FATE SERIES

Believe in the Magic of Christmas

PREVIEW

Chapter 1
Emma Flynn

SOME WOULD DESCRIBE the Houston Galleria at Christmas as a magical place, pulsing with the excitement that came with that final week leading up to Christmas.

The hub of it all was the ice-skating rink.

At the moment, the ice-skating rink itself was closed for a live concert with an up and coming musicians who was currently entertaining the crowds with loud, lively Christmas music blasting from the oversized speakers. The music spilled down the wide halls and into the stores.

The fifty-five-foot tall artificial Christmas tree was adorned with 450,000 twinkling lights and 5,000 ornaments. Every year the artificial tree was hand fluffed by a team of volunteers, the whole process starting in October.

In addition to the tree, giant sparkly ornaments hung from the ceiling turning the whole three-story shopping arena into a holiday wonderland.

The first floor, in addition to the ice-skating rink, housed a hair salon, a Mexican restaurant, a hamburger place, and several fast food restaurants. Other eateries came and went.

During the holidays, there were pop up coffee shops and doughnut shops along with booths selling t-shirts, jewelry, and customized gifts like mugs and teddy bears.

Tourists flocked from all over the world just to come here to shop at the Galleria.

They could get everything from the most expensive jewelry in the country to the latest fashion. Legos. Barbies. Handbags.

There was no excuse for a person to not walk out with the perfect gift.

But it happened all the time.

People came in, looked around, got overwhelmed, and walked out with a gift card. Maybe to a specific store. Maybe a gift card they could spend at any place in the Galleria.

I understood those and they had their place.

According to my sister, a gift card was THE best gift. Hands down.

Like me, my sister loved to shop and being gifted a gift card was better than any actual gift. It was a chance to go shopping. The gift that led to shopping, she called it.

My sister and I both agreed and disagreed in that respect.

Personally I believed that knowing a person and going to the trouble to pick out the perfect gift for them—something they would cherish—something they would know was chosen specifically with them in mind—was better than any gift card.

So I braved the crowds in search of those perfect gifts, one for my sister, of course. I'd slip in a gift card to one of her favorite stores along with whatever gift I found for her. She was truly the easiest person to buy for.

I also had to get gifts for my mother, my father, my grandmother, and my aunt.

Some years I came shopping with an idea in mind about what I was going to get. Last year I had come shopping with an itemized list, everything already figured out.

This year I was shopping into the dark. I had absolutely no idea what I was going to get anyone.

Part of it, I thought as I slipped past a young family with three bright-eyed preteen girls. Everything was bright and shiny and new to them.

They still believed in the magic of Christmas.

I was twenty-seven. It was a little hard to still believe in magic at twenty-seven.

Last Christmas had been different. Last Christmas I'd had a completely different outlook on life. I'd been engaged to a perfectly fine accountant that I thought myself in love with. This year I was supposed to be a married woman. But right in the middle of summer during the brutally hot month of July, Edward, his name was Edward, had broken up with me.

He hadn't even had the decency to offer an explanation.

The breakup still stung, but mostly I considered myself to be over him and mostly when I really thought about it, I was relieved that he was no longer in my life.

He had been one of those guys who preferred to spend time with his friends over spending time with me, especially if it involved my family.

He knew I was close with my family going in. The longer we were together, the more resentful he became about me spending time with my family, even though he was always invited.

Yes. It was definitely best that he was no longer in my life.

I had dodged that bullet.

I ducked into a high end clothing store on the second floor. Wandered the aisles, running a hand over silky dresses and cashmere scarves.

My mother was retired. She had no need for silky dresses and she had a cashmere scarf already, that I had given her that she never wore.

To her credit she kept it, folded and stashed neatly in the top drawer of her bureau along with other things my sister and I had given her over the years.

Maybe that was one point for my sister. Maybe my mother would have preferred a gift card that she could have used to get something else. Something practical like a new pair of walking shoes.

My sister preferred casual and athletic. Nothing in here for her either.

I left the clothing store. There were no other shoppers in the store and, to me, that was a red flag. I preferred, especially at Christmastime, to shop in the crowded stores.

It was probably a silly, even invalid sentiment, but it was my own measure of how good a store was. I had come to the conclusion that people only flocked to the best stores.

I stopped at one of the little coffee shops and bought a latte. Maybe a little caffeine would get my creative juices flowing.

Standing at the railing overlooking the skating rink, I checked in with my sister.

ME: *Are you finding anything?*

After a couple of minutes Zoe wrote back.

ZOE: *Found a couple of gifts. Want to have lunch?*

ME: *Sure. Meet me at the Mexican place?*

I slipped my phone back into my pocket and laughed to myself.

At least Zoe was trying to shop for gifts. She was probably buying gift cards, but that was okay. She put time and energy into buying gift cards from places people would like, so that couldn't be minimized.

The thing that I found most amusing was Zoe's love of eating. She barely weighed a hundred pounds, but she ate any chance she got. Not that she ate much at the time. She just ate often.

I took my coffee and continued to wander down the hallway. I stepped into a high end souvenir store and considered getting my father a t-shirt for him to wear when he and Mother started traveling next year.

The t-shirt had a saying on it.

Home is Where the Heart is... and My Heart's in Texas

I decided to think about it. I could always come back to it later. Part of the fun of shopping was finding things and then deciding what to come back to.

Right now I was in what I called the exploration stage.

There were still six shopping days until Christmas. So I had plenty of time to make last minute decisions.

I stepped onto the crowded elevator with back-to-back people —a woman with a baby carriage, a couple with a child, and several other people—and rode down to the first floor.

The musician had finished her concert and her crew was packing things up. The skating rink staff was busy getting the rink ready to let skaters back out on the ice.

With the musician leaving, the crowd was thinning out a bit, making it easier to walk about.

I gave my name to the hostess at the Mexican restaurant, took a pager, and went back to sit on a bench in front of the skating rink.

They were letting skaters back on the ice now.

For now, however, only the experienced skaters were allowed out on the ice. Performing for the lingering crowd.

They were using them as part of the entertainment.

They were letting Olympic quality skaters entertain people who had come to see the musician.

It wasn't a bad thing. Professional level skaters like that enjoyed getting out on the ice in front of an audience.

They spend most of their lives training for something just like this. This was their chance to get out there on the ice, pleasing the crowds. Taking a bow when they were finished.

It was good practice in case any of them every did make it to the actual Olympics. It could happen. It had happened. We'd had a Houston girl make it. Two of them, in fact.

I watched the skaters with envy. My parents hadn't deemed ice skating worthy of the time and expense it would have taken to send my sister and me to lessons.

Learning to ice skate was not an easy endeavor. It wasn't something just any family could handle.

It was a full-time job that began in childhood and took a commitment from the entire family.

No. I was probably better off doing what I was doing.

It would have been awesome though to have been able to step out onto the ice and wow anyone who happened to be watching.

I straightened in my wool coat. I was okay doing what I did.

My life had plenty of meaning and not a little bit of recognition.

I was, after all, at the top of my field.

"Hey you," my sister said, coming up behind me. "Please tell me we're in line."

I held up the pager. "Shouldn't be long."

"Have you bought anything?" she asked, sitting down beside me, dropping her two shiny red shopping bags at her feet.

"Not yet," I said.

Straightening her coat, Zoe looked at me quizzically before turning her attention to the skaters on the ice.

"Something is wrong with this picture," Zoe said. "I've bought three gifts. Actual gifts. Not gift cards. And the super shopper herself has bought nothing."

"I still have time," I said. "Besides, if all else fails, I know that at least one person would be okay if she got a gift card."

"What's the world coming to?" Zoe asked with a sigh.

"I honestly don't know," I said. "But don't worry. I'll find something. I'll find something for everyone. I'm not giving up yet."

Unfortunately, I felt far less optimistic than I let on.

I'd give it a couple of days, but I might just end up getting everyone gift cards after all.

I didn't want to admit it, but maybe my Christmas spirit was lagging a bit this year.

Chapter 2
Emma

"I'm going to sign you up for a dating app," Zoe announced over tacos.

I picked up my napkin and looked at the stubborn set to my sister's jaw.

"No," I said. "You are not."

"It's been, what? Six months? Since you went on a date."

"I don't have time to date."

The server refilled our glasses of hand-squeezed strawberry lemonade. The lemonade was one of the main reasons I liked coming here.

Zoe sipped her lemonade through a straw.

"Are you sure you don't want a margarita?"

"A margarita sounds good, but you know I'm driving."

"As always," Zoe said as a token complaint. "What don't you just try one of the dating apps?"

"Why don't I not?"

Zoe checked her phone.

"How many of those apps are you on?" I asked.

"A lady never reveals her number," Zoe said primly.

Refraining from further comment, I scooped up a bite of freshly made guacamole.

"Look," Zoe said, holding up her phone. "There are so many guys out there looking for dates."

She showed me a picture of a guy who was unarguably nice to look at.

But in support of the stand I was making, I wrinkled my nose.

She swiped to the next picture.

"How about... a guy with a beard?"

"I don't—"

"Oh look. This guy has a dog."

"I don't know... I'm more of a cat person."

"Picky much?"

I shrugged. "You're the one looking."

Holding up her phone, she scrolled through some more photos.

"You're wasting your time," I said. "I'm on a dating moratorium."

Zoe rolled her eyes. "That's not a thing."

"It's a thing."

"Suit yourself." She laid her phone on the table, the dating app still open to a guy wearing a black turtleneck. No thank you.

"I'll be right back," Zoe said. "Restroom."

"Take your time."

I broke a chip in half and glanced back at Zoe's phone. The guy with the turtleneck smiled up at me, upside down. No... and no.

After I used my napkin to wipe my mouth, my gaze was drawn back to Zoe's phone.

At first I thought the lock screen had come up, but then I realized the photo had changed.

Was it supposed to do that? I wasn't familiar enough with dating apps to be able to answer that question.

Using one finger, I turned her phone around so I could see the picture that was now on her screen.

It was still the dating app, but a different guy.

When the screen started to fade just before it locked, I tapped it to keep it awake.

While I was at it, I pulled it closer.

No. Way.

Absolutely. No. Way.

Zoe slid back into her chair.

"Caught you," she said.

"No."

The look on my face must have alarmed her.

"What is it?"

"Does it change by itself?"

"What do you mean?"

"If you just let it sit there, does it go to the next person?"

"Not unless you swipe it," she said, leaning over to look at her phone.

I looked at my sister, my thoughts going in about fifty different directions.

"I didn't touch it."

"It's okay. I don't mind."

I grabbed her phone and held it up for her to see the image.

She frowned at the screen.

"Is that...?"

"Yes," I said, turning the phone back so the screen faced me.

I studied the blue eyed man with the little smile on his full lips. Smooth skin and a strong chin. Short dark hair.

Wearing a... baseball uniform?

My whole system felt like it just shorted out.

Just shorted out and went on the blink.

Everything about him was familiar.

I knew what it felt like to be on the other end of that blue-eyed gaze.

I knew what it felt like to kiss him.

I knew what it felt like to be in love with this man quite simply because I had never stopped.

Believe in the Magic of
Christmas
PREVIEW

Chapter 3
Emma

"No," I said.

"You have to let me sign you up so you can talk to him," Zoe insisted.

"Not going to happen."

The server cleared off our table and left the check as my sister and I read Theodore Devereaux's dating profile.

"It doesn't really sound so much like him," I said.

"It sounds like him to me," Zoe said.

I bit my lip and read the profile again. It described him, but it didn't sound like anything he would write.

I knew Theodore. I knew just how private he was.

He would never tell anyone that he enjoyed reading science fiction fantasy novels. I'd discovered it by accident. It wasn't like anyone cared, but at the time he had a couple of friends who probably would have ribbed him about it.

And yet there it was right there on the screen.

I like reading science fiction fantasy novels.

But Zoe was probably right. He'd probably gotten over it. He was a grown man now.

It had been ten years since I had seen him.

And yet... if he was on social media, I hadn't found him. Yes, I might have looked. Who wouldn't? Everyone looked for their old boyfriends or girlfriends on social media at some point.

But if he wasn't on social media, then it was quite possible that he was still private. No matter what anyone said, people did not change that much.

Ten years.

At least it would be ten years in five months.

Close enough.

I remembered our last Christmas together.

I'd known something was bothering him then, but I hadn't realized the significance of it. It was only in retrospect that I figured it out.

"Can I borrow my phone?" Zoe asked, holding out her hand. "I need my credit card."

"Of course."

I handed her the phone and watched as she slipped her credit card out of the back cover and swiped it.

We took turns buying each other meals when we went out. I lost track, so had to just assume that it was her turn.

"Do you want the app on your phone?" she asked. "Just in case."

"No," I said shaking off the haze I seemed to have fallen into.

"Here," Zoe said. "I just sent you a screen shot so you can have his picture."

"I don't need—" My phone chimed with a text from Zoe.

"And I just got a warning for violating the app's terms of service," she said with a little shrug.

"For taking a screenshot?"

"Yep. They're very strict. But this was an exception."

"I don't need a picture of Theodore."

"At least you know what he's doing now," she said.

"I knew what he was doing." But it was just a hunch. I hadn't actually kept up with him.

I was surprised he didn't show up on Google.

If he was a baseball player, how could I not have found him?

"Ready to get back to shopping?" Zoe asked.

"Sure." But I was pretty sure shopping was the last thing I wanted to think about right now.

Everyone in my family just might be getting a gift card from me this year, after all.

Believe in the Magic of Christmas

PREVIEW

Chapter 4
Emma

Zoe and I got back to Maple Creek just as the sun was setting over the horizon.

Zoe had an early day tomorrow where she worked in a bakery downtown.

I didn't have an early day, but I had some things I wanted to think about.

After dropping Zoe off at her apartment, I drove to my grandmother's little cottage on the other side of the little town.

The little town of Maple Creek was decked out for Christmas. Colorful lights were strung everywhere. Across every street. Around every door and window. Garland and red bows landed on everything that didn't move and some things that did.

The wooden boxes of ivies lining the sidewalks glowed with twinkling lights.

As I drove through town, I heard Christmas music spilling from the speakers.

The stores were closing for the evening. So different from Houston where the stores stayed open into the night, especially during the holidays.

I had mixed feelings about being back here in Maple Creek, but it had been my choice.

My grandmother was getting up in age and she needed someone to help her take care of things around the house.

Since I worked from home, it was easy enough for me to relocate.

Granted, my sister could have moved in with her, but Zoe didn't have the temperament. And besides that, she was rarely home.

"Grandma, I'm home," I called as I went in through the back door.

"Good," Grandma said. "I could use some help with hanging up the clothes."

"You did the laundry?" I asked. "That's supposed to be my job."

"If you take all the jobs, what am I supposed to do?"

"Just do your thing. Exercise. Watch television. Talk on the phone."

"I did all those things today." Grandma waved a hand dismissively. "I even made some cookies."

"You aren't supposed to use the kitchen." I automatically walked over and checked to make sure all the burners were off.

The last time Grandma had cooked something, she'd forgotten to turn off the oven.

"Don't worry," she said. "I remembered to turn the oven off."

"I know you did." But it didn't keep me from worrying.

"You got a box in today. You ordered something?"

"Just some supplies," I said.

I walked through the house, making sure everything was as it should be.

Whiskers, the cat, had a bowl full of food. His water bowl fountain was full, water tumbling out of the fountain.

Grandma, it seemed, had taken care of everything she was supposed to do while I was in Houston with my sister.

I filled a glass with water and sat down at the kitchen table with her.

"What kind of cookies?" I asked, picking one up.

"Chocolate chip," Grandma said proudly.

"Your old recipe," I said, taking a bite. "As good as I remember."

Grandma beamed.

"What did you do all day?" I asked. "Besides make cookies."

"I took a walk with Doreen. You know all she does is talk. About nothing. I swear I've never known anyone who talks as much as Doreen and never says anything of any importance."

I hid a smile. Sometimes Grandma and her friend Doreen were mistaken for twins.

"We stopped at the Piggly Wiggly for a few groceries. They have their Christmas stuff on sale."

"Sounds like you had a big day."

"Oh," she said, obviously remembering something. "You had a phone call."

I instinctively glanced at the cell phone in my hand. No calls.

"On your home phone?" I asked.

"Yes. He said he'd call back."

My stomach did a little flip. Grandma'd had the same phone number since I was a little girl.

"Who was it?"

"He didn't say. But he sounded like a nice young man."

I didn't give anyone Grandma's home phone number. I used my cell phone only.

Who would try to reach me at Grandma's house?

"It was probably a wrong number," I said, picking up a second cookie. Grandma wasn't supposed to be using the kitchen, but she hadn't lost her knack for baking.

Zoe had most definitely gotten her passion and skills for baking honestly.

Maybe it had been a wrong number. It had to be.

But I couldn't help thinking that the only person who could possibly know where to find me here was... Theodore.

Keep Reading
Believe in the Magic of Christmas...

Kathryn Kaleigh writes sweet contemporary romance, time travel romance, and historical romance.

kathrynkaleigh.com

9 798330 679119